The Cat

Georges Simenon

The
Cat

Translated from the French by Bernard Frechtman

A Helen and Kurt Wolff Book
Harcourt, Brace & World, Inc., New York

The Cat

I

He had let go of the newspaper, which first unfolded on his lap and then slid slowly over his knees before dropping to the waxed floor. One would have thought he had just fallen asleep were it not that a narrow slit could be seen between his eyelids from time to time.

Was his wife taken in by this? She was knitting in her low armchair on the other side of the fireplace. She never seemed to be observing him, but he had known for a long time that nothing escaped her, not even the barely perceptible quivering of one of his muscles.

The steel jaws of the crane opposite crashed heavily against the ground near the concrete mixer with a clanking din. The shock shook the house each time, and each time the woman started and put her hand to her chest as though the noise, to which by now she must have been used, reached to her very vitals.

They were observing each other. They had no need to look at each other. They had been observing each other that way for years, slyly, constantly refining their game with new subtleties.

He was smiling. It was five minutes to five according to the black marble clock with bronze ornaments, and one might have thought he was counting the minutes, the seconds. Actually, he was counting them mechanically, he too waiting for the big hand to be vertical. The noises of the mixer and the crane would then suddenly stop. The men in raincoats whose faces and hands were dripping with rain would be motionless for a moment before heading for the wooden shed that had been put up in a corner of the lot.

It was November. Since four in the afternoon they had been working by the illumination of floodlights that would be turned off in a moment, and then, without transition, there would be darkness and silence. The alley would be lit up only by a single gas light.

Emile Bouin's legs were numbed by the heat. When he opened his eyes, he saw the flames, some of them yellow and the others bluish at the bottom, spurting from the logs on the hearth. The fireplace was made of black marble, like the clock and the four-branched candlesticks on either side of it.

Except for Marguerite's hands and the faint clicking of the knitting needles, everything in the house was silent and motionless, as in a photograph or a painting.

4

Three minutes to five. Two minutes. Workmen were beginning to trudge to the shed to change their clothes, but the crane was still functioning and a last jawful of cement rose up to the framing that marked the first story of the structure.

One minute to. Five o'clock. The hand quivered hesitantly over the pale face of the clock, and then five spaced gongs rang out as if everything in the house had to be slow.

Marguerite sighed. Her ear was alert to the sudden silence outside that would last until the following morning.

Emile Bouin was thinking. Smiling vaguely, he watched the flames through the slit of his eyelids.

One of the logs, the one on top, was now only a blackened skeleton from which streaks of smoke rose up. The other two were still glowing, but the crackling announced that they were going to collapse before long.

Marguerite wondered whether he would be getting up, to take a couple of fresh logs from the basket to put in their place. Both of them were accustomed to the heat from the hearth and did not move their chairs back until the skin of their faces actually stung.

His smile broadened. He wasn't smiling at her. Nor at the fire. He was smiling at a thought that flashed through his mind.

He was in no hurry to translate it into action. They had time, both of them, all the time that separated them from the moment when one of them would die. How could one tell who would go first? Marguerite surely thought of it too. They had been thinking of it for many years, several times a day. It had become their main problem.

Finally he sighed too, and his right hand left the armrest of the leather chair and felt for the pocket of his house jacket. He drew from it a little notebook that played an important role in their domestic life. The narrow pages had dotted lines that made it possible to detach neatly strips of paper an inch and a quarter wide.

The cover of the notebook was red. A thin pencil fitted into a leather loop.

Had Marguerite given a start? Was she wondering what the message would be this time?

She was certainly used to it, but she could never know what words he was actually going to write, and he purposely remained motionless a long time, with his pencil in his hand, as if he were thinking.

He had nothing in particular to communicate to her. He merely wanted to upset her, to keep her on tenterhooks, at the very moment when she felt relieved by the end of the din in the lot.

Several thoughts occurred to him, and he rejected them one after the other. The rhythm of the knitting needles was no longer quite the same. He had succeeded in disturbing her, at any rate in arousing her curiosity.

He made the pleasure last another five seconds, during which time they could hear the footsteps of one of the workmen moving toward the end of the alley.

He finally wrote, in block letters:

THE CAT.

Then he remained motionless again for a while before putting the notebook back into his pocket after tearing out a strip of paper.

Finally, he folded the strip up very small, the way children do with a piece of paper that they shoot with a rubber band. He did not need a rubber band. He had become amazingly clever at the game, almost Machiavellian.

He placed the paper between his thumb and middle finger. He cocked his thumb and suddenly shot the message into Marguerite's lap.

He almost never missed. He rejoiced inwardly each time.

He knew that Marguerite would not bat an eyelash, that she would pretend to have seen nothing, would continue to knit, moving her lips as if in prayer while she silently counted the stitches.

She sometimes waited for him to leave the room or turn his back in order to put fresh logs on the fire.

At other times, after a few minutes of apparent indifference, she would let her right hand slide over her apron and pick up the message.

Although their acts were always more or less the same, they did occasionally introduce variants. Today, for example, she waited until all the noises from the lot had stopped, until silence invaded the alley at the end of which they lived.

She put her knitting down on a stool as if she had finished her work, and, with her eyes half closed, she too seemed about to doze off, lulled by the warmth of the logs.

She then pretended, much later, to notice the folded

paper on her apron and picked it up with her delicately wrinkled fingers.

It looked as though she were going to throw it into the fire, as though she were hesitating, but he knew that that was part of the daily play-acting. He was no longer taken in.

Children play the same game every day at the same hour over a more or less long period of time, and they do so without losing their apparent belief in what they are doing. They act "as if."

The difference here was that Emile Bouin was seventy-three years old and Marguerite seventy-one. Another difference was the fact that their game had been going on for four years and that they did not seem to tire of it.

In the warmth and silence of the living room, the woman finally unfolded the paper and, without putting on her glasses, read the two words that her husband had written:

THE CAT.

She did not turn a hair. There had been longer, more unexpected, more dramatic notes, some of which were veritable riddles.

This note was the most trivial, the one that recurred most often, when Emile Bouin could think of nothing more clever.

She threw the paper into the fireplace where a thin flame shot up and died immediately. With both hands on her stomach, she sat there motionless; the only life in the living room was that of the hearth.

The clock quivered and struck once. Marguerite stood up as if at a signal. She was small and slender.

Her woolen dress was pale pink, the pink of her cheeks, and the checked apron was light blue. There were still blond glints in her white head of hair.

Her features had sharpened with the years. For others, for those who did not know her, they expressed gentleness, melancholy, resignation.

"Such a long-suffering woman! . . ."

Emile Bouin did not snicker. Both of them were beyond such obvious manifestations of their states of mind. A shudder, a curl of the lip, a fleeting gleam in the eyes— these were sufficient.

She would look around, as if hesitating about what to do next. He would sense her move, as one foresees one's opponent's move when playing checkers.

He had not been wrong. She was walking over to the cage, a big white and blue standing cage with gold bars.

A multicolored parrot was perching motionless on a bar and staring fixedly, and it took a good moment or two to realize that the eyes were made of glass and that the parrot was stuffed.

She nevertheless looked at it tenderly as if it were still alive, and, moving her hand forward, she slid a finger between the bars.

Her lips were moving, as they had been a while before when she was counting her stitches. She was speaking to the bird. One almost expected her to feed it.

He had written:

THE CAT.

She was replying silently:

THE PARROT.

The classic answer. He was accusing his wife of having poisoned his cat, his own cat, which he had loved long before he knew her.

Every time he was seated by the fire, dulled by the waves of heat from the logs, he was tempted to reach out and stroke the furry, black-streaked animal that used to curl up in his lap as soon as he sat down.

"A common alley cat," she would maintain, in the days when they still spoke to each other, almost always in order to start an argument.

Though the cat was not pure-bred, it was not an alley cat either. Its long, supple body glided along the walls and furniture like the body of a tiger.

Its head was smaller and more triangular than that of the domestic cat and its gaze was intense and mysterious.

Emile Bouin claimed that it was a wild cat that had ventured into Paris. He had found it as a kitten in a construction plant at the time he was still working for the Paris Highways Department.

He was a widower and lived alone, and the cat had become his companion. At the time there were still private houses on the other side of the alley where a big apartment building was now going up.

When he had crossed the street to marry Marguerite, the cat had followed him.

THE CAT.

The cat that he had found one morning in the darkest corner of the cellar.

The cat that had been poisoned by eating the food that Marguerite had prepared for it.

The animal had never got used to Marguerite. During the four years he had lived in the house opposite, it had never accepted food from anyone but Bouin. Two or three times a day, its master would signal to it by simply clucking his tongue, and it would follow him on the sidewalk of the alley as if it were a trained dog.

He was the only one who had ever stroked that cat until the day they entered a new house in which there were unfamiliar smells.

"He's a bit shy, but he'll get used to you."

It had not got used to her. It was mistrustful and never approached either Marguerite or the cage of the parrot, a big brightly colored macaw that did not speak but that uttered horrible cries when it was angry.

Your cat . . .

Your parrot . . .

Marguerite was gentle, almost bland. One imagined her young and slender, already dressed in pastel tones and strolling poetically on the bank of a river with a parasol in her hand and a big straw hat on her head.

Besides, there was a photograph in the dining room that showed her like that.

She was as thin as ever, except that her legs had swollen a little. She faced life with the same too-sweet smile that she had formerly put on for the photographer.

The cat and the parrot, which were equally mistrustful, observed each other from a distance, and with a certain respect. When the cat began purring on its master's knees, the parrot would stop moving and observe it with its big round eyes as if it were perplexed by that regular and monotonous sound.

Had the cat discovered the power it had over the macaw? Did it watch the bird with quiet satisfaction through its half-closed eyes?

It was not in a cage. It shared the pleasant warmth with its master, who protected it.

A moment would come when the parrot, tired of studying a problem to which there was no solution, would become irritated and angry. Its feathers would quiver, its neck would grow tense, as if there were no bars around it, as if it were going to swoop down on its enemy, and the house would resound with its piercing cries.

Marguerite would then say, "You'd better leave us for a moment. . . ."

"Us" meant herself and her bird. The cat would quiver too, knowing that it was going to be picked up and carried into the cold dining room, where Bouin would sit down in another armchair.

Marguerite would open the cage and speak in tender tones, as if to a lover or a son. There was no need for her to extend her hand. She would go and sit down again in her chair. The macaw would look at the closed door of the living room and listen to assure itself that there was no danger, that the two strangers, the man and his animal, were no longer there to threaten it or make fun of it.

Then, with a great leap, it would fling itself onto the back of a chair, for it did not fly. In two or three hops, it would reach its mistress and alight on her shoulder.

She would go on with her knitting. The play of the

gleaming needles fascinated the bird. When it had enough, it would rub its huge beak against the woman's cheek and then on the softer skin behind the ear.

YOUR CAT.

YOUR PARROT.

The minutes would flow by, with Emile in the dining room and Marguerite in the living room, until it was time to prepare dinner.

In those days, it was still she who did the cooking for both of them.

At the beginning, Emile had continued to prepare the food for his cat. One week when he had the grippe and had stayed in bed for three days, she availed herself of the opportunity to buy lung at the butcher's, cut it up into small pieces, cook it, and mix it with rice and vegetables.

"Did he eat it?"

She had hesitated.

"Not immediately."

"Did he finally eat?"

"Yes."

He was almost sure that she was lying. The following day he had a high temperature, and she said the same thing to him. The next day, while she was out marketing on Rue Saint-Jacques, he went downstairs in his bathrobe and found the food of the previous night under the sink. It was untouched.

The cat, which had followed him, had looked at him reproachfully. Emile had mixed the food again and offered the plate to the animal, which did not make up its mind at once.

When Marguerite got back, she found the plate empty. The cat was not on the ground floor, but in the bedroom upstairs, lying against its master's legs.

That was where it slept every night.

"It's not hygienic," she had protested the first few nights.

"It slept with me for years, and it didn't make me sick."

"Its snoring keeps me from sleeping."

"It doesn't snore. It purrs. One gets used to it. After all, I got used to it."

She was partly right. The cat did not quite purr like other cats. Rather, it made a snoring sound, which was as sonorous as that of a man who has drunk too much.

Now, standing near the cage, she would stare at the stuffed parrot and move her lips as if she were talking to it tenderly.

Emile, whose back was half turned to her, had no need to see her.

He knew that game just as he knew Marguerite's other games. He smiled vaguely, still gazing at the charred logs. Finally, he got up, took two new logs, and put them into the fireplace, arranging them with the help of the tongs.

Outside it was now quiet except for the pattering of the rain and the thin jet of the fountain in the marble basin. The alley contained seven houses, side by side, all exactly alike, with a door in the middle, two windows at the left, those of the living room, and at the right the window of the dining room, behind which was the kitchen. The bedrooms were on the floor above.

Two years earlier, replicas of these houses, the even-numbered ones, stood on the other side of the street. The enormous iron ball of the demolishers had knocked them down as if they were cardboard toys, and the entire view now consisted of a workyard cluttered with cranes, girders, steam rollers, planks, and wheelbarrows.

Three residents of the street had a car. Even with the blinds closed, one could hear if someone went out in the evening. And from outside one could tell in which room the people were sitting.

Few tenants drew their curtains, and one could see families at table, a man with thinning hair reading in his armchair under a tarnished picture frame, a child bent over a notebook and sucking its pencil, a woman peeling vegetables for the next day.

Everything was mild, soft, muted. Actually, one really heard the fountain only once one was in bed and had put out the light.

The Bouins' house, which was still called the Doises' house, was the last in the row, against the high wall that closed the alley. At the foot of the wall was a statue, a bronze Eros holding a fish. A thin jet of water that spurted from the fish's mouth fell into a marble shell.

Marguerite had gone back to her chair in front of the fire. She had stopped knitting. Wearing her silver-rimmed glasses, she was turning the pages of the newspaper which she had picked up from the floor near her husband's armchair.

The black hands of the clock advanced slowly, trembling hesitantly on the hour and half hour.

Emile was not reading or looking at anything. He sat there with his eyes closed, perhaps thinking, perhaps dozing, and occasionally shifted the position of his legs because of the heat.

When the clock struck seven, he stood up slowly and, without looking at his wife or at the cage of the stuffed parrot, walked to the door.

The hall was not lit. The entrance door, in the middle of which was an empty letterbox, was at the left, and the stairway leading to the first floor, at the right. He switched on the light, shut the door behind him, and opened the door to the dining room, with its cold, stagnant air.

The house had central heating, but it was turned on only on very cold days. Besides, they no longer used the dining room. They ate in the kitchen, where the gas stove gave a feeling of warmth.

Bouin, who was careful and methodical, put out the light in the hall, closed the door behind him, walked to the kitchen, and, when the light was on there, turned off the light in the dining room.

He had adopted his wife's economical habits, and he had an additional reason for doing what he did.

He knew that Marguerite had started squirming in her chair as soon as he had stood up. She did not want to follow him too closely. She was waiting a little. When she got up with a sigh, she would have to extinguish the lamps in the living room, put on the light in the hall, then extinguish it, and also shut each door behind her.

These movements of each of them had become ritual gestures and had a more or less mysterious meaning.

In the kitchen, Emile Bouin took a key from his pocket before opening the cupboard on the right, for there were two cupboards. The one on the left, which was older, had already been there in the time of Marguerite's father.

The one on the right, which was painted white, had been bought by Bouin on Boulevard Barbès.

He took from it a cutlet, an onion, and three cooked endives, which were left over from lunch and which he had put into a bowl. He also took a half-empty bottle of red wine and poured himself a glass before attending to his butter, oil, and vinegar.

After lighting the gas, he melted a scoop of butter, sliced the onion, and, when it began to brown, put the cutlet in the frying pan.

Marguerite had appeared in the doorway, pretending not to see him and to ignore the fact that he was there, to ignore even the smell of the onion.

Taking a key from her belt, she opened *her* cupboard.

The room was not large, and the table occupied a good part of it. They had to move carefully to keep out of each other's way. They were so used to it that they hardly ever grazed each other.

They no longer used a tablecloth but made do with the checked oilcloth.

Marguerite also had her bottle. It did not contain wine, but a cordial that had been popular at the beginning of the century and that her father had given her at lunch and dinner when she was still an anemic girl.

On the label, which was old-fashioned, were unidentifiable leaves and ornate lettering: Cordial of the Alps.

She poured herself a tiny cordial glass and wet her lips with relish.

When the cutlet was cooked and the endives were reheated, he put the food on a plate and sat down at one end of the table in front of his bottle, his bread, his salad, his cheese, and his butter.

Apparently indifferent to what he was eating, she spread her dinner at the other end of the table: a slice of ham, two cold potatoes which she had wrapped in foil before putting them into the refrigerator, and two thin slices of bread.

Her husband was ahead of her. One of them would sometimes sit down to eat when the other had already finished. It did not matter, since they ignored one another.

They ate in silence, just as they did everything else. Bouin was sure that his wife was thinking: "There he goes eating meat twice a day again! And he fries onions on purpose."

It was partly true. He liked onions, but he did not necessarily want them every day.

At times, in order to make her angry, he would prepare complicated dishes for himself, dishes that would take an hour or two to cook. This had meaning for him. It proved that he had not lost his appetite, that he still was an epicure, that he didn't mind attending to his food himself.

Some mornings he would bring back tripe, the mere sight of which disgusted his wife.

In the evening, as if to emphasize her frugality, she would make do with a slice of ham or cold veal, a bit of cheese, and at times a potato or two left over from lunch.

That had a meaning too. Several meanings. In the first place, it established the fact that he spent more money on food than she did. Secondly, that she refused to use the frying pan after him. When it was necessary, she would wait for him to clean it, even if it meant eating much later.

They chewed slowly, she with barely perceptible movements of the jaws, like a mouse, and he, on the contrary, noisily manifesting his appetite and pleasure.

"You see! Your presence doesn't disturb me in the least. . . . You thought you were punishing me, that you were getting the better of me. . . . Well, I'm very happy, and I haven't lost my appetite."

Of course, their dialogues were silent, but they knew each other too well not to divine every word and every intention.

"You're a vulgar man. . . . You eat sloppily and you stuff yourself with onions like a common person. . . . As for me, I have always had a bird's appetite. . . . That's what my father called me. . . . His little bird. . . . And my first husband, who was a poet as well as a musician, called me his fragile dove."

She would laugh, not outwardly. Inwardly. Her laughter was no less apparent.

"It's he, poor thing, who died. . . . He was the fragile one. . . ."

Her gaze would glide over her second husband and would harden.

"And you who think you're so strong, you'll go before I do too."

"I'd have gone long since if I hadn't been careful. . . . Remember the bottle in the cellar?"

Now it was his turn to laugh, inwardly. Despite the fact that they were alone in the silent house and had condemned themselves to muteness, they nevertheless indulged in fierce repartee.

"Just wait . . . I'm going to spoil your dinner for you."

He took the notebook from his pocket, wrote four words, detached the strip of paper, and skillfully tossed it onto his wife's plate.

She unfolded the note without surprise.

CAREFUL ABOUT THE BUTTER.

It was more than she could take. She stiffened. She had never been able to get quite used to that particular joke. She knew that the butter was not poisoned, since she kept it under lock and key in her cupboard even though it got soft and sometimes runny.

She nevertheless hesitated to eat any more of it and managed to do so only at the cost of an effort.

She would take revenge later. She did not yet know how. She had time to think about it. Neither of them had anything to do.

"You're forgetting that I'm a woman and that a woman always has the last word, just as a woman lives three to five years longer than a man. All you need do is count the widows. . . . They're far more numerous than widowers."

He had been a widower, but it was by accident, it didn't count. His wife had been run over by a bus on Boulevard Saint-Michel. She had not died at once but had dragged on helplessly for two years. He was still working. He had not yet retired. When he returned in the evening, it was to take care of her and look after the house.

"She took her revenge, didn't she?"

An emptiness. Silence. The rain in the yard.

"I sometimes wonder whether you finally didn't get tired of it and end by getting rid of her. . . . With all the medicines she took, it was easy. . . . She wasn't as careful, as shrewd as I am. . . . She was a nobody, with big red hands, who had milked cows in her youth. . . ."

Marguerite had not known her. The couple had lived in Charenton. It was Emile who had spoken to her about the red hands, had spoken tenderly about them, at a time when they were still on speaking terms.

"It seems odd to me to see you with such white hands, such delicate joints, with almost transparent skin. . . . My first wife was a country girl, well built, with sturdy red hands."

He would take from his pocket a package of Italian cigars, the black, twisted, very strong kind known as coffin nails.

He would light one, puff a blast of pungent smoke into the air, and use the match to pick his teeth.

"A lesson for you, old girl. . . . That'll teach you to be so delicate."

"Wait. . . . You'll get all that's coming to you."

He would empty his wine glass, finish the bottle, then, after a moment of immobility, lumber to his feet and go to the sink, where he would turn on the hot water.

While she finished her meal in dainty mouthfuls, he would wash his dishes, clean the frying pan, first with a piece of paper and then with a cloth, and carefully wrap the bone and fat of the cutlet in an old newspaper which he then threw into the garbage pail under the stairway. Not forgetting, of course, to lock his cupboard.

A slice of the day had thus been nibbled away, and he tackled the last slice by going back to the living room and turning the knob of the television set. It was time for the news broadcast. He would change the position of his chair. The logs on the hearth were almost burned out, but it was no longer necessary to look after the fire, for the room was now filled with a pleasant warmth.

Then she would wash her dishes. He would hear her moving about. She would join him, but she would not turn her chair toward the television set immediately. The news did not interest her.

"It's all dirty politics, accidents, and brutalities," she used to say.

She would pick up her eternal knitting. Then, when a program of songs was announced, she would shift her chair, first slightly, then a little more, and then completely. She did not want to seem too greatly interested in such nonsense. Nevertheless, she sometimes wiped her eyes during a sentimental, sad romance.

Bouin got up to take the garbage can and put it at the

edge of the sidewalk. The rain was icy. The alley was lonely with its seven houses in a row, its few lighted windows, the three cars that were waiting for the following morning, and that awful workyard where walls were beginning to loom up beside gaping holes.

The fish in the fountain kept spitting its jet of water into the shell, and the bronze Eros dripped with rain.

He locked the door behind him and shot the bolt. Then, as he did every evening, he lowered the blind in the dining room and then the one in the living room where the television was on.

It was only a silvery gleam, but that gleam enabled him to see in a flash that his wife had a thermometer in her mouth.

She had managed! It was her little revenge, her riposte to the matter of the butter. She imagined that she was going to worry him by making him think that she was sick.

In the past, she had spoken about her chest, her bronchitis, and at the slightest drop of temperature she had wrapped herself up in shawls.

"You can croak, old girl."

He did not just think that. He wrote it on a slip of paper which she received in her lap when she wasn't expecting it. She read it, removed the thermometer from her mouth, looked at her husband pityingly, and then, taking a piece of paper from her pocket, she wrote:

YOU'RE GREENISH ALREADY.

She did not throw it, but laid it on the table. Let him be inconvenienced. She did not fortify herself with a notebook of detachable slips. Any old bit of paper would do, even a piece of newspaper.

He would not dare to get up immediately. Despite his curiosity, he would wait as long as possible.

She found the way to make him move. All she had to do was get up and turn on another station. He would not stand having to listen to a program other than the one he had chosen.

So, as soon as she got back to her chair, he stood up, switched the channel, and, in passing, picked up the note as if accidentally.

Greenish! He laughed. He laughed on purpose. He laughed badly, not quite heartily, for it was true that he did not have a good complexion. He noticed it every morning when he shaved.

At first he blamed it on the light in the bathroom with its frosted glass. He had looked at himself elsewhere. He had, of course, lost weight. When one gets older, it's better to get thin than fat. He had read in the paper that insurance companies make fat men pay a heavier premium than thin ones.

All the same, he had difficulty getting used to the man he had become. He was tall. In the past, he had been broad, heavy, husky.

On the job, he had worn huge boots and, in summer as well as winter, a black leather jacket. He ate and drank whatever he pleased, without bothering about his digestion. For more than fifty years, it had never occurred to him to weigh himself.

He now felt skinny in his loose clothes, and occasionally

he felt a pain, sometimes in a foot or a knee, sometimes in his chest or at the back of his neck.

He was seventy-three years old, but, apart from growing thin, he refused to consider himself an old man.

And she—did she consider herself an old woman? When he got undressed, she would look at him mockingly, without realizing that she was in much worse shape than he.

Another of their games! They would play it later, around ten o'clock, when they would go upstairs to go to bed. There were three bedrooms on the upper floor. The night of their marriage, they had quite naturally slept in the same one, which had been the bedroom of Marguerite's parents and the one she had shared with her first husband.

She had kept the old oak bed, the feather mattress, and the enormous quilt. Bouin had tried to get used to them. After a few days, he had given up, especially since his wife refused to sleep with the window open.

He had not gone so far as to change bedrooms. He had brought his own bed and set it up next to his wife's.

The wall was covered with flowered paper. At first, there were only two enlarged photographs in oval frames on it, one of Marguerite's father, Sebastian Doise, and one of her mother, who had died of tuberculosis when Marguerite was still a small child.

Later, when they had stopped speaking to one another, Marguerite had put up, next to her father, a photograph of her first husband, Frédéric Charmois. According to the photo, he was a slim, distinguished-looking man, with a poetic air about him. He had a thin mustache and a pointed beard. He was first violinist at the opera and gave lessons to a few pupils during the day.

Less than a week later, Bouin responded to the provocation by hanging up a picture of his first wife at the head of his bed.

Thus, each flouted the other, as they seemed to flout each other when they undressed. They could have gone to another room, but they did not want to change in any way the habits of the early years.

Bouin almost always undressed first, as discreetly as possible. Nevertheless, there was a moment when he showed his naked chest, his ribs, which stood out more and more, and his hairy legs and thighs, from which the muscles had melted away.

He knew that she was watching him, delighted to see him withering away, but a little later it was his turn to glance furtively at his wife's flat, skinny chest, her drooping buttocks and swollen ankles.

"You're a sight, my dear girl!"

"And you, you think you're handsome?"

They still did not speak to each other. They measured each other in silence. Each went to brush his teeth in turn, for the bathroom was the only room in the house where they were never together.

Bouin would get into bed heavily and put out his bedside light. His wife would slip between the sheets more delicately. And he knew that she kept her eyes open for a long time waiting for sleep to come.

He fell asleep almost immediately. Another slice of the

day, the last one, was consumed. Tomorrow would be another day, pretty much the same.

It was good to sleep. It was particularly good to have dreams in which he was ageless, in which he was not old. He would sometimes see landscapes as he had seen them in the past, landscapes that were alive, with vibrant colors, landscapes that smelled good. At times he would even run until he lost his breath in search of a spring whose murmur he could hear.

He never dreamed of Marguerite, and rarely of his first wife, and when he did it was always of her as she had been shortly before their marriage.

Did Marguerite dream too? About her first husband? About her father? About the time when she wore broad-brimmed straw hats and strolled along the Marne under a parasol?

What did it matter to him? Let her dream about her first husband the musician and about her childhood if she felt like it.

He didn't care, did he?

II

He woke up at six o'clock, as he did on other days, as he had done all his life without ever using an alarm clock. His father, too, always got up early. He was a mason, at a time when cranes were not yet used in building and when walls went up brick by brick.

They lived in a small house in Charenton just behind the lock that linked the Marne canal to the Seine. People in the neighborhood thought that his father had gray hair because it was sprinkled with plaster and mortar.

There was no bathroom in the house. They washed in the yard, near the pump, bare-chested in winter and summer alike, and once a week, on Saturday, they went to the public baths.

Bouin had been a mason too. He had started as an

apprentice at the age of fourteen, and his work had consisted chiefly in buying bottles of red wine for the entire crew.

He went to night school. He didn't get much sleep. He was already married when he took his foreman's examination and then, much later, his examination as building inspector.

The name of his first wife was Angèle, Angèle Delige. She came from a village near Le Havre; when she was sixteen her parents sent her to Paris, as they had done with her four sisters. She had been a nursemaid, and then a salesgirl in a delicatessen.

It was true that she had milked cows and that she had big red hands.

They had rented an apartment not far from the lock, on Quai de Charenton, and in those days Bouin still went to hug his father and mother every morning before going to work.

There was no bathroom on Quai de Charenton either. He continued going to the public baths, the corridors of which were invaded with a steam that had a human smell.

"Why don't you use the bathtub?"

He was sixty-five when he remarried, and she sixty-three. They were very awkward with each other, more intimidated than very young lovers.

Were they really in love?

"I prefer showers. . . ."

To be stretched out in warm water filled him with anguish. He felt as if seized with a numbness that did not seem natural. He preferred to soap himself under the shower and then to run cold water over his naked body for a long time.

"Are you going to go on getting up so early when you have nothing to do all day long?"

To him, the bed was somewhat like the bathtub. He felt comfortable in it at night and sank quickly into sleep. But at 6:00 A.M., and often earlier in the summer, he felt the need to return to life. In order to please her, he had tried to linger between the sheets, but it gave him an uneasy feeling in the chest.

He would get up noiselessly and make his way to the bathroom, where he would shut the door and bolt it. After showering and shaving, he would slip on a pair of old corduroy trousers that were too big for him, a flannel shirt, and go downstairs in his slippers so as not to make any noise.

He was convinced that she was awake, that she pretended to be sleeping, that she was listening attentively to every sound.

In the kitchen, he prepared a big bowl of coffee for himself. After making sure that he had his key in his pocket, he went to the entrance door and went out to the alley.

At that time of year, it was still dark, and the lamppost was the only source of light.

For years his cat had followed him with an almost solemn pace, as if that stroll in the empty streets was an important act to him, a kind of mass which they both celebrated in silence.

Bouin did not have a cat on Quai de Charenton. During

the last two years of his wife's life, when the accident had crippled her, he had no time to go walking. He looked after the house, put things away, washed, scrubbed, prepared Angèle's breakfast.

Before the accident, he spent at least a half hour strolling along the quays, observing the canal boats, the barrels that were to be delivered to a big wine-dealer, the tugs coming from above Corbeil which drew four or five barges of sand.

He now invariably made the same tour. The alley branched out from Rue de la Santé, halfway between the prison and Cochin Hospital. Lower down was the insane asylum, which he passed before going up Rue du Faubourg Saint-Jacques.

At the corner of Rue de la Tombe-Issoire and Place Saint-Jacques, he would see St. Dominique's Church, where Marguerite went to mass on Sundays. In the summer, she sometimes went on weekdays too.

There was a time when she received Holy Communion every morning. In those days she was very friendly with the priest, whom she helped decorate the altars and to arrange the flowers in front of that of the Virgin.

What had come between them? What had been the cause of their quarrel? The fact remained that she had stopped seeing him and taking part in parish affairs. Instead of occupying a personal pew, she contented herself with a rush-bottomed chair at the back of the church.

Except for the day of his marriage, Bouin had entered the church only once, out of curiosity. He had been baptized. He had received his first communion. But nobody in his family went to mass, which had not prevented his father and mother from having religious funerals.

He had only one sister, who had got off to a bad start in life. For years the family had been without news of her. They did not know whether she was living or not. Then one day, a letter that had been forwarded to various addresses, with an envelope containing comments by various postmen, had finally reached Emile. His sister informed him that she was married to a miller from the neighborhood of Tours, that she had two children, a big house on the banks of the Loire, and an American car.

He had not seen her again. He had merely written, saying that he was a widower and that he was nearing retirement age.

He would turn to the right on Avenue du Port-Royal, then right again on Rue de la Santé, which was always as empty as when he had left it.

In the course of a fifteen-minute stroll, he passed a hospital, a prison, an asylum, a school for nurses, a church, and a firehouse. Wasn't this a kind of summing up of life? The only thing lacking was the cemetery, which was not so very far away.

When he returned, one of the neighbors, Victor Macri, who had a solemn gait, would be emerging from number 3 and starting his car. They would exchange greetings. First the car would let off smoke before the motor gradually got into its stride, and Macri would head for the big hotel on the right bank where he was a porter.

Marguerite and he knew all the residents of the alley. Marguerite was the owner of the row of houses that remained. A few years before his death, her father had sold the opposite row where a big apartment house was now rising.

Emile Bouin took the key from his pocket. After three years, he still missed his cat, and almost every morning he hesitated slightly as if to let the cat in first as he used to do.

He would hear footsteps on the upper floor, the water flowing into the bathtub. He would raise the blinds. Before long, the darkness outside would be less dense, the light from the lamppost would grow pale, and he would hear a slamming of doors and footsteps moving toward Rue de la Santé.

Neither the loneliness of the hour nor the emptiness around him weighed upon him. All his life, he had been in the habit of going through the same routine at given times.

Certain gestures, certain schedules, had changed. He had known different periods, but each had been marked by a definite rhythm, which he avoided breaking.

It was now the time, as it had been when he got ready to go out on a job, for red wine, bread, and salami.

His father, before leaving for work, used to eat a big bowl of soup, a beefsteak, or a stew, which did not keep him from taking food along for a midmorning snack.

His mother was small and rather stout. He mainly remembered her doing the laundry, which she then hung up in the yard. There were no washing machines. Even if they had existed, they would have been too expensive. And probably his mother would have been scared by them as she was scared by everything that was electrical.

She would put the clothes to boil in a huge galvanized kettle, and she had to start her washing early, because she needed her husband or son to help her remove it from the stove before leaving.

There were the ironing days, the evenings devoted to mending socks, the afternoon for the copper pots, with the result that the week was a succession of different images and smells.

Curiously, as he grew older he became almost insensitive to smells. Nor did he see the streets as he had seen them in the past, when they offered a constantly changing spectacle of which he never wearied.

He had then had the impression, when he plunged into the crowd, of being part of a whole, of participating in a kind of symphony, each note of which, each spot of color, each gust of heat or coldness, enchanted him.

He could not have told when the change had taken place. No doubt gradually, as he aged, without his being aware of it. For he had never realized that he was getting older. He did not feel old. He was really amazed when he thought of his age.

He had not become wiser, nor more indifferent. He still had the thoughts and odd ways and made the gestures of the youngster he had been.

On Place Saint-Jacques, he had bought the morning paper, which he glanced at while eating. Marguerite spent a long time upstairs washing and dressing. Three years earlier, when they spoke to each other, he had pointed out to her that it was dangerous to bathe in a locked room, for she might have a fainting spell and nobody would realize it.

It had become a habit of his, even though they were at war, to cock his ear while she was in the water. This was easy because the bathroom was directly above the kitchen. The drainpipe went through the kitchen, to the right of one of the cupboards, and made a racket every time the tub emptied.

He would drink two glasses of wine, from a thick glass, as in the country. He would drink a third glass later, around the middle of the morning, when he got back from his marketing.

It was 7:15 by the alarm clock. He had the impression that its ticking was louder in the morning than during the rest of the day. He had also noticed that it was quicker than that of the clock in the living room. He wondered why, since they kept the same time.

He would light his first Italian cigar and go down to the cellar, which was lit by a very weak bulb that hung from the ceiling. For about a quarter of an hour he would cut wood, for it was more economical to buy it in big pieces than already cut to the dimensions of the fireplace.

He would fill the basket and take it up to the living room. Then there was the delicate job of lighting the fire while listening to the news broadcast on a portable radio.

Actually, the news did not interest him. It was a habit, a pebble to mark one step in the unfolding of the day. He would hear Marguerite enter the dining room and then the kitchen. Outside, the rain fell in a whitish fog.

35

He did not have to keep an eye on her, since his food was under lock and key in his cupboard. She would then prepare her coffee, caffeine-free coffee, for she was convinced that she had a heart ailment.

Or was it only an alibi, a reason for complaining or for assuming sickly expressions?

She would have her coffee with three or four buttered rusks, and therefore she had hardly anything to wash up afterward.

The fire would begin to take the chill off the living room. Although the daylight was still dismal and indecisive, he put out the lights and went upstairs, where he had to make his bed. He made the bed carefully, without leaving a crease in the sheets, blankets, or counterpane.

Marguerite would then go up. They did not greet each other, did not exchange a look. Each went about his business, glancing furtively at the other only when they believed themselves unobserved.

She was aging. To be sure, she was no longer a young woman when he met her but middle-aged, and somewhat delicate, which perhaps added to her distinction.

She had a clear, pink complexion beneath her silky white hair, and her face had a gentle, kindly expression.

The storekeepers on Rue Saint-Jacques adored and respected her. She did not belong to their world, but to a world apart. She was a kind of aristocrat in the neighborhood where her father had built the houses in the alley that was named after him.

For more than thirty years, she had lived with a man as distinguished as herself, a musician, an artist, the first violinist at the opera, who could be seen at night in a black cape and evening clothes and who for a long time had continued to wear a top hat.

He too had that vague, gentle smile, that politeness which was both shy and a shade condescending.

"He's such a good teacher. . . . This year again, one of his pupils got first prize at the Conservatory."

At that time, in the alley one could hear for hours on end the same musical phrases being repeated by a violin which the professor accompanied on the piano.

The piano was still in a corner of the living room, encumbered with photographs and fragile curios. Marguerite had played it until the death of her first husband, and when she returned from the funeral she had decided that she would never touch the instrument again.

Bouin had insisted at first. She would answer with gentle obstinacy:

"No, Emile. It was his piano. . . . It's still a little of his life. . . ."

He had once lifted the lid and run a finger over the ivory keys. She had come rushing down, indignant and unable to understand how he could have been so bold.

In her eyes, the piano was part of her husband. It was a holy relic, as was the violin which was locked in a closet. Of course, another man now shared the bedroom that Frédéric Charmois had occupied with her for more than thirty years. He washed in the same bathroom. In the beginning, they had tried to have the same intimate relations.

Things had not worked out. They were both intimidated and had the impression that at their age the gestures which they made so awkwardly were ridiculous, that they were a kind of parody.

Who knows? Perhaps Marguerite regarded it as a sacrilege. She would lie there with her eyes closed and her lips tightly pursed. She was resigned. Since they were married, her new husband had the rights to her body.

But that body remained stiff, on the defensive.

"Why don't you go on, since you want to?"

"How about you?"

"I don't know."

Perhaps she had felt like it, before. Perhaps on falling asleep at night she sometimes dreamed of pleasures which she had known in the past. At the moment of resuming them, her feelings rebelled.

"We'll get used to it. . . ."

They had tried several times.

"I thought you loved me."

"I do love you. Forgive me. . . ."

"What's holding you back?"

"Forgive me," she would repeat. "It's not my fault."

And tears would tremble at the edge of her eyelashes.

Instead of working out, things had got very bad. As soon as he approached the oak bed, he would see Marguerite's body shrink away, her eyes become harder, almost hostile.

He was the male, the brute who thinks only of his personal satisfaction. She had already suffered from his heavy step, the way he moved about the house where formerly everything had been discretion and delicacy. She had never quite got used to his cigars, which, in the beginning, he had smoked in the doorway.

As for the cat, it inspired her with an almost superstitious terror.

On the very first day, the animal had stared at her as if it were trying to understand why she was butting into their shared existence.

It would sometimes follow her through the house and up the stairs as if to assure itself that she was not a threat, and its golden eyes, which were full of mystery, seemed always to be asking questions.

It slept on Bouin's bed, against his legs, where, before letting itself fall asleep, it waited for that strange creature who slept in a neighboring bed to be completely motionless.

At that period, Marguerite alone looked after the house.

"Aren't you going to take your walk?"

She did not like to see him wandering about the house while she was cleaning. He would take his coat and go walking in the streets, sometimes far away, for example, along the quays, which he sometimes followed with his even gait as far as his former neighborhood.

He was neither happy nor unhappy. He would stop to have a glass of wine in a small café, as in the past, when he would go off for a drink during the morning break.

The difference was that formerly he was surrounded by people like himself, who were covered with dust or mud. They would speak loudly, they would laugh, the glasses would clink.

"This round's on me, Alice!"

He had worked for a long time in the very center of town when Boulevard Haussmann was joined to the Grands Boulevards. He had also taken part in the transformation

39

of the outer boulevards when the former ramparts were demolished.

Wherever they were, the workers would discover a cozy little bar where they met several times a day. Often they ate there, taking their food from their knapsacks. His first wife, Angèle, found that life quite natural. They had no children and did not try to know whether it was his fault or hers.

Angèle was not distinguished. She was gay, noisily so. She loved the movies. She sometimes went alone in the afternoon, and often, in the evening, she asked him to go with her to see another film. On Saturday nights, they went dancing.

In the summer, on Sundays, they took a train to the nearby countryside. They met friendly couples and drank with them.

They were warm, they sweated, they bathed in the river. Angèle did not know how to swim and splashed about near the shore.

On the way home, they would have a funny taste in their mouths, the taste of the fried food which they had just eaten, of the mud of the river. Their heads would spin a little, for they had drunk rather heavily. His wife's hand on his arm felt heavier as they approached the house.

"I'm dizzy."

It amused her to feel drunk.

"Aren't your legs wobbly?"

"No."

"I bet you'll want to make love."

"And why not?"

"I'd like it too, but I don't think I'm up to it. Your hard luck if I fall asleep. . . ."

Nothing was important. Nothing was serious, nothing was dramatic. Sometimes the meal wasn't ready or the bed was unmade.

"Just imagine, I slept almost all day. It's your fault too. If you hadn't been at me until two in the morning . . ."

Marguerite would have found her vulgar. She was, but it was a good and healthy vulgarity and resembled her husband's.

"Tell me, have you ever slept with other women?"

"Occasionally."

"You still do it?"

"From time to time, when there's a chance. There are almost always young women prowling around the jobs."

"Aren't you ashamed to take advantage of them?"

"No."

"Is it the same with them as with me?"

"Not quite."

"Why?"

"Because I love you. With the others it's like having a drink."

"If they knew what you think of them . . ."

"They don't worry. Sometimes we pass them on to one another. . . ."

Who knows, perhaps Angèle deceived him too. He preferred not to think about it, but he did not reject the possibility. She was free in the afternoons. She would go into town and visit the shops, not to buy, because she could not afford it, but for the fun of it. Every movie poster tempted her, and she would go off to sit in the darkness.

Didn't any man try his luck then? Not only old ones, for whom it's a kind of disease, but young ones who had the day off?

"Have you ever cheated on me?"

"Why do you ask that?"

"Because you've just asked me the same question."

"Do you think I'm going to give the same answer? Are you jealous?"

"Perhaps I am. Perhaps not. . . ."

"What would be the point? You're enough for me, aren't you?"

It was not an answer. He would sometimes think about the matter and scowl, but he could not be said to be anxious.

Maybe yes, maybe no. Anyway, she was a fine girl who did her best to make him happy.

He was happy. He had no desire for change. He was satisfied with his life. Later perhaps he would buy a car and go driving with Angèle on Sunday instead of taking the train or bus.

He did not foresee that his wife would be run over one autumn afternoon on Boulevard Saint-Michel or that, when the time came to retire, at the age of sixty-five he would marry a woman almost as old as he.

By ten o'clock he would finish his share of the household work. She had not asked him to help. It was he who had decided, the day after they had stopped speaking to one another, that he would not be indebted to her. At that time, their anger was still hot. They would sometimes mutter in a low voice. Each felt himself a victim and regarded the other as a monster.

Almost in a fury, he had begun to clean the living room, dining room, and even the kitchen, where he got on his knees and washed the floor with soapy water, as he had seen his mother do in the past.

Because there was only one vacuum cleaner, he had to wait until he no longer heard the noise of it in the bedroom, which was Marguerite's domain, to go and get it. Strict justice would have required that she give it to him halfway down the stairs.

Once a week he waxed the living-room floor, not in order to give pleasure to the old woman but because he liked the smell of the polish.

It was after that that the little game began. It had just begun. He did not like the word "game." Marguerite probably did not like it either. But how did she refer, in her own mind, to what took place every morning?

The word "game" implies a certain gaiety which neither of them felt, except from time to time, and which they were very careful to hide.

Seen from another point of view, their actions and gestures were tragic or grotesque rather than comical.

This morning, Marguerite had not forgotten the comedy which she had begun the night before with the thermometer. She had it in her mouth again when he went up to get the vacuum cleaner. Her hair was covered with a pale blue kerchief as it was every morning. Was her color really bad? Was it the light of this rainy, foggy day? The air outside was slightly yellow.

And what if she really got sick? She had never been sick, in spite of her complaints. He had never been really sick either, and they both seemed destined to live to a ripe old age.

Marguerite on the upper floor and he on the ground floor were now waiting to see who would leave the house first. He had already put on his mud-colored raincoat and his rubbers. His cap was within arm's reach.

She must have been ready too. The day before, he had lost patience and had gone out with a shrug of his shoulders.

Today, after a ten-minute wait, which she had no doubt spent, ready to leave, with her umbrella in her hand, standing in the bedroom, she decided to go down and get her shopping bag in the kitchen.

He had one too, almost the same as hers. The street door shut behind his wife, and then he too left the house.

He saw her on the sidewalk, small and slender, clumsy on her swollen legs when she tried to avoid puddles of water, with the purple umbrella swaying above her head.

She knew that he was following her. On other days, it was she who trailed him, never at a great distance, for he was careful not to walk too fast.

She turned to the right toward Boulevard de Port-Royal and crossed the street opposite Cochin Hospital, where there were ambulances in the yard in which interns in white smocks moved about rapidly.

A little later they would enter, separated by a distance

of a hundred feet, the busy Rue Saint-Jacques, where the stores were full of housewives.

He was asking himself, "Is she going into the grocery store?"

Rossi's grocery was an Italian shop. The store was dark and deep and overflowing with food. It specialized in prepared hors d'oeuvres, small artichokes in oil, fried fish in a spicy sauce, and marinated octopus about an inch long of which Emile was very fond.

He needed sugar and coffee. When he entered, Marguerite was looking at the shelves and ordered spaghetti and three cans of sardines.

She did not look as if she knew he was there. They ignored each other in public as well as at home, and the local storekeepers had got used to seeing them enter one behind the other without so much as looking at each other.

Every man for himself. Nevertheless, they spied on each other, and if one of them ordered something expensive or original, the other tried to outdo him.

"Have you got any cannelloni?"

"Freshly made this morning."

"Give me four."

They were long and generously stuffed. She must have started.

"Let me have three slices of Parma ham," she said. "Not too thick. I have such a small appetite!"

She wore a shawl under her coat, like someone who does not feel well and is afraid of catching cold. It also made her look older, more broken-down with age.

"Aren't you well, Madame Bouin?"

People always hesitated to call her by that name. The old-timers had known her first as Mademoiselle Doise. That name had great glamour for them, for they sold Doise Biscuits and Doise Cookies.

It was Marguerite's grandfather who had created the biscuit factory whose tall smokestack with a capital D painted in white halfway up still stood on Rue de la Glacière.

Here, among the metal boxes with glass covers that contained cookies, were several boxes with the name "Doise," followed, it is true, by the mention: "V. Sallenave, Successor."

For more than thirty years, too, they had called her Madame Charmois, and they had never quite got used to her present name of Bouin.

Madame Rossi was waiting on her.

"Anything else, Madame?"

"Let me look at my list. Do you still have the same chocolates you had last time?"

"Those with hazelnut filling?"

"That's right. I'll have half a pound. I only take one occasionally. . . . So they last a long time."

As for him, he did not forget the sugar and coffee. He added a quarter of a pound of salami and of mortadella. Unlike his wife, he felt no need to furnish explanations.

Marguerite was taking coins from her purse.

"How much do I owe you?"

He lingered in front of the shelves so as not to approach the cash desk until the moment she was leaving.

A few steps farther was the butcher shop. The clients

lined up. Raoul Prou joked with the housewives as he cut up his meat.

Emile waited until two customers had lined up behind Marguerite before he entered the shop.

What was said about them when they left? It was unthinkable that Prou, in any case, did not make any comments.

"See those two nuts? They're husband and wife, and every morning they arrive one behind the other looking as if they didn't know each other. Each buys for himself. . . . I wonder what they do all day long in their house. . . . But she was a fine woman. Her first husband played the violin at the opera and gave lessons. . . ."

"It's your turn, Madame Bouin. . . . Have you got a cold?"

"I think I'm beginning to come down with bronchitis."

"Be careful. . . . Mustn't play around with that kind of thing at your age. . . . What will you have today?"

"Let me have a little veal cutlet, very thin. . . . You know . . ."

He knew. She spoke to them all about her birdlike appetite, as if to avoid the accusation of avarice.

"Please trim the fat."

"There won't be much left."

"It'll be quite enough for me."

They must have pitied her, must have blamed him for the situation. When he married her, he still looked like a husky brute, for it was only recently that he had begun to shrivel. He smoked his strong little Italian cigars. He would spit a yellowish jet of saliva on the ground, and he could be seen going into cafés for a drink. Marguerite's first husband would never have behaved in that way!

And didn't some people maintain that he had managed to put one over on her, and that he had married her just for her money?

That was false. He was about as rich as she was. There was no telling exactly, for she was discreet about such matters. When they had married, she had retained legal control of her own estate, but she did not seem to have any direct or indirect heirs.

As for him, in addition to his savings he had his pension, and if he died before her she would receive three quarters of it for the rest of her life.

Which of the two, therefore, was self-seeking?

Both of them? Either?

"Have you got a nice veal kidney?"

She had opened her purple umbrella as she left the butcher shop and headed for the dairy.

He joined her there while she was paying. He had not seen what she had bought. He knew only that it had cost her two francs, forty-five centimes.

"A quarter of a pound of Münster cheese."

A cheese that had a strong smell and that she loathed.

"A dozen eggs."

He would buy a quarter of a pound of mushrooms and that evening, before the cheese, he would prepare a creamy, lavish omelette, the kind he liked. She would look disgusted. Perhaps she would leave the table, as she sometimes did, especially when she saw him unwrap the Münster.

She was standing in front of the stall of the vegetable dealer, from whom she was buying potatoes. She loved potatoes, whether hot or cold, and ate them at almost every meal.

"Let me have a quarter of a pound of mushrooms."

He did not add, as she would have done: "It's for an omelette."

"Anything else, Monsieur Bouin?"

He needed potatoes too, and he had the dealer put them at the bottom of the bag so that they would not crush the other things.

"Some onions . . . Preferably red ones. . . ."

"Shall I give you half a pound? They keep very well."

"I know. . . . Some parsley . . . Two pounds of potatoes . . . Not those . . . I prefer these, a little shriveled. . . ."

The shopkeepers must have thought that he remained a gourmet and continued to indulge himself while his poor wife merely nibbled a few crumbs.

He did not need anything else. He watched his wife enter the drugstore with the green front, and he saw the pharmacist showing her several boxes and tubes of pills, no doubt medicines for a cold. She was asking questions, hesitated, and finally chose lozenges. That was not all. She also bought something which he recognized from afar. Mustard plasters.

That evening, before going to bed, she was going to apply one to her chest, after moistening it. Then she would twist and squirm in order to place a second one on her back. It was difficult. He pitied her each time, and he was tempted to put out his hand to help her, but he knew that she would have regarded such a gesture as an insult.

Then, while the two plasters were producing their effect, she would nervously walk back and forth between the bedroom and the bathroom until the pain became unbearable.

She was capable of keeping them on for a long time. One would have thought that it was a self-imposed punishment, and when she removed the mustard plasters her skin was as red as a fresh wound.

Was that all, this time? No, she also wanted to exchange a book at the secondhand bookstore which exchanged volumes for fifty centimes. She invariably chose novels of the beginning of the century, sad stories that contributed to her melancholy.

He would glance at a few paragraphs when she was not in the living room. There was always a proud, courageous victim who suffered every possible misfortune but who nevertheless kept her head high.

"Poor woman . . ."

He often thought that. He, too, sometimes regarded himself as a brute. Then he would start brooding over the memories of the last three years and would end by writing a little note:

THE CAT.

It was doubtless she who had put rat poison into the animal's food. She had taken advantage of his being in bed with the grippe.

In the evening, he had been surprised that the animal had not jumped on his bed.

"Have you seen him?"

"Not since this afternoon."

"Did you put him out?"

"I opened the door for him at about five o'clock, when he wanted to go out."

"Did you stay outside with him?"

It was midwinter. A crust of snow covered the pavement of the alley. The demolition work across the way had not begun, and the two rows of houses faced each other as in the time when Sebastian Doise had constructed them.

"Hasn't he scratched at the door since?"

"I haven't heard anything."

He was already beginning to get out of bed.

"Don't you want me to go and see?"

"I'm going myself."

"Are you going outside in spite of your fever?"

It seemed to him that there was something false in his wife's voice. Until then, he had found her complicated, often tormented by fixed ideas, some of which were a bit silly, but it had never occurred to him that she might be vicious.

It was the cat, and the cat alone, that had become the object of her bitterness. Every time it touched her, she would jump aside and let out a scream. She overdid it. He was convinced that she was putting on an act. During the very first week of their marriage, she had insinuated that he might get rid of the animal by giving it to friends, for example.

"I've been afraid of cats all my life. I might perhaps get used to a dog. We had one, when my father was alive, and it used to follow me around when I was little and seemed to protect me. Cats are treacherous. You never know what they're thinking. . . ."

"Joseph's not like that."

For Joseph was the name he had given the animal that he had found one evening on his way home.

That shocked Marguerite.

"I don't think it's right to give an animal the name of a saint."

"It's too late to debaptize it."

"How can you utter that word? As if one baptized animals!"

"Why not?"

That had been their first quarrel. There had been others, all of them about Joseph, who listened to them as if it knew what they were discussing.

"He's not even pure-bred."

"Neither am I."

That was to tease her. It was part of his character, one of his habits. On the job, the men were pretty rough with each other, which did not prevent them from going off and drinking together when the whistle blew.

With Angèle, too, he spoke quite freely, and sometimes went rather far.

"Come here, mulehead."

"Why do you call me mulehead?"

"Because you're like all women. To look at you, one would swear that you run yourself ragged to satisfy me, that nothing counts but me. In reality, you're like a mule, you do exactly what you feel like doing."

"It's not true. I always obey you."

"In a sense, that's true. When you feel like doing something, you convince me that I'm the one who wants it. Don't deny it, old girl. . . . Go on, I know you! You're as big a slut as the others."

"Aren't you ashamed?"

"No."

They would end by bursting out laughing and, most often, by rolling on the bed.

With Marguerite, it was different. There was no question of rolling on the bed or of using coarse language. Crude words made her shudder, and she would immediately withdraw into silent disapproval.

She still went to communion every morning, and late in the afternoon she would sometimes kneel in the dark church, near a confessional.

"Well, did you go off to pray?"

"I prayed for you, Emile."

He did not hold it against her. Rather, he was annoyed with himself for having married her, for he was not the man to make her happy.

How did the idea ever occur to him? He had often thought about it. Which of the two had made the first advances?

He lived opposite her, on the spot where the crane was now set up. He had taken a room on the upper floor of the home of a young couple for whom the house was too large and the rent too high.

That was why he had left Quai de Charenton. He felt lost in the apartment which he had shared with his wife. Usually he ate in a restaurant. A big room and a bathroom were enough for him. His armchair was near the window, from which he could hear the water in the fountain. In the evening, when he did not go out, he watched television.

He had made some friends at the café on Place Denfert-Rochereau where he went to play cards. As for women, there was always Nelly, even though it wasn't very comfortable. He attached little importance to the matter.

In the morning, he would see the little lady from the house opposite go shopping, and he found her distinguished. She resembled the women on old-time calendars with their gentle smile of resignation.

He knew that she was the owner of the opposite houses, that was all. Although he knew her name, he did not associate it with the cookies that he had eaten when he was a child.

They would return home, she with her umbrella and shopping bag which would sometimes knock against passers-by, and he with his small cigar and his face wet with raindrops.

They would find themselves in the same quarters, each with his thoughts, each with his little packages, waiting for the time to prepare lunch.

On Place Saint-Jacques he would stop and, letting her go on ahead, would go into a bar for a glass of red wine.

The boss's wife served at the counter. She was as old as Marguerite and had a hard bun on top of her head and big flabby breasts that hung down above a big stomach.

"It looks as if it's going to snow," she said, looking at the color of the fog.

He had gone downstairs, with his woolen bathrobe over his pajamas and his bare feet in his slippers. He had looked everywhere, in the living room, in the dining room, in the kitchen, and, what with his fever, he finally got a headache as a result of bending down to look under the furniture.

From time to time he would emit the faint whistle to which the cat was accustomed, and he would sometimes call out, in a gentle voice in which anguish was apparent:

"Joseph . . . Joseph . . ."

Then he had put on his rubbers and slipped on over his bathrobe the first thing he found on the coat hanger, the old black leather vest. He didn't give a rap about looking ridiculous.

"Emile!" called his wife from the top of the stairway. "Don't go out. It's bad for you."

Nevertheless, he went through the alley, in the darkness, over the crackling snow, and he almost slipped and fell on the sidewalk two or three times. At the lighted window of one of the houses, the second one, a child watched him with its face glued to the pane and then turned around to call its mother, who could be seen through the open door of the kitchen.

His outfit frightened children. He walked to Rue de la Santé. When the cat was let out to attend to its needs, it never went beyond the invisible line that separated the street from the alley.

"Joseph!"

He felt like crying. He would never have thought that the absence of the cat could move and distress him to such a point.

Two dogs lived on the street, a brown dachshund that belonged to a spinster and a Pomeranian that a twelve- or thirteen-year-old girl took out on a leash. There had never been any trouble between them and Joseph. When the latter met them, he disdainfully looked elsewhere and, if necessary, stepped off the sidewalk to let them go by.

He had left the door ajar. He pushed it open, took off his leather jacket and rubbers, and went up to the bedroom. His gaze was hard and his features were drawn. As he was about to get into bed, he thought of the cellar and went downstairs. Marguerite, visibly nervous, followed him to the ground floor.

"Did you get wood?" he asked her.

"I had to heat the house, after all. . . ."

He did not yet accuse her, but he was beginning to suspect her. In the cellar, he lit the feeble bulb and began to search among old boxes, bottles, and logs.

"Joseph!"

He found it, at the very back, against the damp wall, behind a pile of firewood. The animal was stiff, its eyes open and motionless, its body twisted. It seemed much thinner than when it was alive. Slobber had stuck under its mouth, and there was greenish vomit on the ground.

Emile took it in his hands and vainly tried to close its eyes. The contact with the almost icy body had given him a curious sensation in his spinal column.

He was not a quick-tempered man. He had, on rare occasions, got into fights, especially in cafés, only once on the job, and each time he had kept his self-control.

But now his face had an evil look. Holding the animal in his hands, he looked around as if searching for something. And he found it.

There were many rats in the alley. At times they could be seen prowling at night around the garbage pails, and Marguerite was very afraid of them.

"Do you think we have any in the cellar?"

"It's possible."

"If I were sure, I'd never dare go down again."

He had bought a product with an arsenic base that was sold everywhere. From time to time, in the evening, he would spread it on slices of bread and leave them in a corner of the cellar.

All he had ever found was the corpse of a single rat,

an enormous one, to be sure, almost as big as Joseph. Perhaps others had gone to die elsewhere.

The metal container of the rat poison was kept on a crude shelf where they put various objects that had no place elsewhere.

He put the cat down for a moment, struck a match, and saw the former circle that the container had left on the dusty wood. There was another circle.

Picking up his dead cat, he had gone upstairs, slowly, so slowly, so heavily, that Marguerite on the ground floor must have felt the menace.

She wanted first to take refuge on the upper floor, but as he barred the way she rushed into the living room. When she tried to lock the door, he moved his foot forward, forced his way in, went up to her with the same slow gait, and, with his left hand, grabbed her hair.

At the same time, with his right hand he raised Joseph's corpse in front of the frightened face.

"Look, you bitch! Take a good look!"

With her whole body trembling and her eyes bulging from her head, she had cried for help in a shrill voice. She had lost all self-control and looked as if she were insane.

"Emile! Emile! Please, pull yourself together. . . . You're frightening me. . . ."

He continued rubbing the cat's fur over her face until she fell to her knees, then dropped forward, as if she had fainted.

"I know very well that it's an act. Everything you do is

an act, you slut! I wonder what keeps me from going and getting the poison and forcing it down your throat."

He was breathing hard, his head was spinning. He must have been crimson, frightening.

She did not move. And he, in order to release his fury, put out his arm and swept away all the knickknacks and photographs lined up on the piano.

After that, without looking at his wife, he went upstairs, still holding the cat, which he placed delicately on the chest.

His temperature must have gone up. He felt a spell of dizziness. He lay down, put out the light, and remained motionless, with his eyes open.

At first, nothing moved in the house. For more than a quarter of an hour, there was silence. Then there were indistinct noises, scratchings. A door was opened cautiously, then another.

Marguerite had crossed the dining room to go to the kitchen, probably because she felt the need of a shot of her famous cordial. He later found the glass beside the sink.

It was almost an hour before she dared go upstairs, and she waited a while longer listening, with her ear against the door. Finally she entered the bedroom, hesitated, and lay down on her bed without undressing.

Neither of them had slept much. Emile had difficulty breathing. He dozed off several times, and each time he was awakened by nightmares which he vainly tried to remember later.

At six o'clock he opened his eyes for good. His head ached. He almost remained in bed. He had perspired a good deal, and his pajamas and pillow were damp.

His wife was sleeping. She had been incapable of remaining on guard to the very end, and her pose was almost as tormented as that of the cat in the cellar.

He felt drained, unable to think. He slipped on his bathrobe mechanically, took the cat by two paws, as if it were a rabbit, and went down the stairs.

Joseph was no longer a companion, a living thing that had shared part of his life and exchanged so many looks with him. The animal was now only a corpse, an inert thing, which was beginning to smell.

He remained standing in the hallway, finally opened the door, and took three steps to the garbage can. The garbage collectors had not yet come by. Raising the lid, he placed the now limp body in the can.

After that, he washed his hands in the kitchen and prepared his coffee.

He had no doubt about Marguerite's guilt. Wasn't it established by the fear she had displayed when he had gone down to the cellar?

He drank only a few mouthfuls. The coffee sickened him. He stood up, opened his cupboard, and took the bottle of wine that was already started. It was, as usual, red table wine. He drank two glasses one after the other, with his elbows on the oilcloth of the table. It was still a long time before daybreak. It was December, and the night before the sky had seemed heavy with snow.

He first thought of going away. But where? Should he

take a furnished room in a small hotel while waiting to find another apartment? In that case, he had to remove his furniture, put it in storage somewhere.

From his first marriage, he had kept the bed, his armchair in the living room, the television set, and, upstairs, a desk that Angèle had given him. It was a Christmas present. Christmas was approaching again.

He would not accept a gift from Marguerite, who usually gave him slippers or shirts or socks. He would not give her anything either.

It was over between them. She had just revealed herself as she was, as he had often suspected her of really being beneath her saccharine manners.

He poured himself a third glass. He had no desire to be upstairs again with her. Let her sleep. Let her sweat it out. He would never again speak to her.

They were both old, even if they did not realize it in the usual course of events. In a few years they would be dead. Was he, because of a cat that had been picked up in the street one evening . . .

He mustn't weaken. It was not only Joseph who was involved. It was he himself that she had been aiming at through the animal.

As soon as he had entered that house, in fact as soon as they were married, he realized that Marguerite was bent on changing nothing.

A grandfather Doise named Arthur who wore sideburns, a frock coat, and a very high collar had founded the biscuit firm on Rue de la Glacière. Little by little he made a prosperous business of it.

He had only one son, Sebastian, and a daughter, Eleonore, a yellowed photograph of whom was in the blue leather family album.

Eleonore had died at the age of thirteen, of tuberculosis, as did Marguerite's mother later.

When Sebastian married, he was already a corpulent man close to forty who also wore a frock coat with a double watch chain on which charms were suspended.

Little by little, a Doise state of mind had been created, a Doise atmosphere, a Doise ritual. The alley had been constructed at a time when buildings were regarded as the safest investment and when whole streets emerged from the ground here and there in Paris and on the outskirts of the city.

Later, Sebastian had ordered the fountain, and the word "alley" had been changed. On the blue and white street plaque, as well as on notepaper and visiting cards, appeared the name Square Sebastian-Doise.

Old Arthur had died. Sebastian's wife had died. All that remained was a daughter, Marguerite, and her father took her walking in her laces and embroidered dresses on the Champs-Elysées and in the Bois de Boulogne.

There existed a photograph of them in a hired carriage. Sebastian did not devote all his time to the biscuit business, as old Arthur had done. He frequented clubs and spent afternoons at the races, wearing a gray derby and with field glasses slung over his shoulder.

Marguerite had a governess, Mademoiselle Piquet. There was a cook in the house and a cleaning woman several days a week.

A young man came to give piano lessons to the young girl, Frédéric Charmois, whom she finally married.

The house seemed safe against any attack from without.

However, a certain Victor Sallenave worked on Rue de la Glacière. He had begun as a bookkeeper for old Arthur. When the latter died, he became increasingly important in the firm and before long brought his son Raoul into it.

Exactly what had happened? Marguerite remained vague and contented herself with allusions to these events. Emile had had difficulty in getting her to admit that two women in the family had died of tuberculosis. When he had asked her whether her father had been a gambler, she had replied with an innocent air:

"Why should he have been a gambler?"

The Doises must remain spotless even once they were dead. All the family stories gradually took on pastel tones. Everything was pure and delicate, like the poetic profile of the violin player.

And yet Sebastian Doise had found himself one day facing bankruptcy, a word even more unmentionable than the word "tuberculosis."

In order to avoid scandal and the inevitable smirch, he had preferred to turn the business over to the Sallenaves, father and son, with the result that Raoul Sallenave, whose father was now dead, was the master on Rue de la Glacière and on the quays of Ivry where he had constructed new buildings.

What was the son of a Charenton mason, what was this brute of a foreman, doing in the house?

Had she not often made him feel the abyss that separated them and that nothing could fill?

She had married him out of the fear of remaining alone, of having no one to look after her in an emergency, because a man was needed in the house, if only to cut and bring up wood and to take out the garbage can.

Perhaps too the aging widow had been stirred by the contact with the male who came for a cup of tea almost every day.

It had been a failure. She had stiffened at their first physical contact, and the two beds were a symbol of their botched union.

In short, he was only an intruder and, in her heart of hearts, she must have accused him of having wormed his way into her life by trickery.

As if it hadn't been she who had called out to him!

He was at his window one hot August morning. When he was with Angèle, he would sometimes take a vacation, go to the seashore or to the country. But since he was a widower, he seldom left Paris. What would he have done all alone, away from home?

Marguerite, across the way, had suddenly opened her door with a dramatic gesture. It was ten o'clock. All through the alley, blankets, sheets, and mattresses were being aired at the windows.

Looking anxiously about, she sought someone whom she could call upon, and she was obviously in a panic.

"Monsieur!" she had cried out to him from the sidewalk.

He had stood up.

"Won't you come down? Please come quickly, because the whole house will be flooded. . . ."

He had come down as he was, without his jacket, and had crossed the street.

"What's happening?"

"A leak in the bathroom . . . I don't know what to do about it. . . ."

He went up the stairs in that house which he did not know but which resembled the one he had just left. A pipe had burst in the bathroom, and a veritable geyser was spurting in an almost boiling stream.

"Do you have tools, a big monkey wrench?"

"I don't think so. . . . No. . . . I've never bothered about those things. . . . There were tools in the cellar, but they were rusty, and I got rid of them. . . ."

"I'll be back in a moment. . . ."

He returned with tools from his own apartment.

"Where's the meter?"

"Under the stairway. . . . Good God! The ceiling's going to be damaged."

Five minutes later, the water had stopped spurting.

"Let me have a bucket and a rag."

The water on the bathroom floor was a few inches high, and, despite the woman's protests, he had carefully sponged it up.

"Please don't bother. . . . I'm ashamed to have called you. . . . Someone I don't even know!"

"Well, now you know me."

"Let me finish the job. . . . That's no work for a man. . . ."

"So that you can get soaked too?"

He worked quickly, without impatience, like a man who had used both hands all his life.

"Do you have a clean towel?"

He set everything in order, and when he had finished, one would have thought that nothing had happened.

"The pipe is old, in bad condition. It probably dates from the time the house was built, and that wasn't yesterday."

Had he irritated her?

"I didn't know. What should I do?"

"I could solder it, but it wouldn't last long. . . . Better change it up to the main. . . . Wait. . . . Ten feet. . . . Fifteen feet. . . . Do you have a plumber?"

"I don't remember ever having needed one, in any case not since the death of my husband. . . . Before that, I didn't bother about those things. . . ."

She seemed so frail, so bewildered, alone in that house, that he had suggested:

"Would you like me to take care of it?"

"Are you a plumber?"

"Not quite. . . . But I know something about such things. . . ."

"Would it be expensive?"

"The cost of fifteen feet of pipe."

They went downstairs one behind the other.

"What can I offer you? Won't you have a drink?"

That day he had made the acquaintance of the famous cordial.

"Don't you like it?"

"It's not bad. . . ."

"When I was a girl, I had to take it against anemia. . . . Just a little glass before lunch . . . I've never been very strong."

That had amused him. He had gone back to his room to change, then he went to a hardware store to buy the piece of pipe. When he rang at the door she had had time to put on an old pink dress and to arrange her hair.

"Back already! Are you sure that I'm not imposing on you? Don't you have other things to tend to?"

"I have nothing to do all day long."

"It's true that I often see you sitting near your window. . . . You live alone too?"

"Ever since my wife died. . . ."

"Don't you work? You used to leave early in the morning and return only in the evening."

"I retired six months ago."

She dared not ask him what he had done before. He had brought a blowtorch and a tool kit, and he had a little more than an hour's work.

"It's so nice of you! A woman alone feels helpless and quite lost as soon as the slightest thing happens."

"If there's another leak, or anything else, don't hesitate to call me."

"How much do I owe you?"

He took the hardware dealer's bill from his pocket. It came to fifteen francs and a few centimes.

"What about your work?"

"You're not going to pay me for that. I'm only too glad to have been able to be of use to you."

"Will you have another drink?"

"To tell the truth, I drink only wine."

"And I who don't have any in the house! Listen . . . Come back this afternoon and I'll have a good bottle. . . ."

"Ordinary red wine will do. . . . I'm not used to fancy labels."

The sun was shining. The two of them were smiling on the threshold.

He did not care to remember it.

He stood there, miserable, in his bathrobe, barefoot in his slippers. The kitchen had not been heated. His nose was running and he constantly had to wipe it.

He had gone to get one of his Italian cigars from the living room, and the tobacco had a bad taste. He had not smoked during the three days he had spent in bed. He had hardly eaten anything.

He had drunk jugs of hot lemonade sweetened with honey that Marguerite brought him. She had prepared custard for him. She was displeased that he refused the mustard plasters which she would have liked to apply, very hot, on his chest and back.

And now? He heard the tap flowing above his head and deduced from it that she had just got up and was brushing her teeth. She must have been afraid. He wondered whether she would come downstairs after dressing.

How many glasses of wine had he drunk? The bottle was empty. He stood up to get another from the cupboard, for there was still only one cupboard for the two of them.

As a rule he drank moderately, and one could count on the fingers of one hand the number of times he had got drunk.

That morning, the blood had rushed to his head. He must have been flushed. It seemed to him that something crucial had happened, something whose consequences he could not yet foresee.

Since Marguerite had poisoned his cat, everything had become false. He had already suspected that things were false between them, though he had not wanted to believe it. He recalled certain images, remembered certain phrases and glances.

They had never uttered the word "love." They were too old for that. Had he really loved Angèle, his first wife, and, despite her smirks and smiles, had Marguerite really loved her first husband?

It was now hard to say which of the two had been the first to envisage a life in common.

They were separated only by the width of the alley. Neither she nor he had known a long solitude. They were both used to being part of a couple.

He was alone in his room, above the young couple which had just had a baby. She was no less alone in a house where she felt somewhat lost, somewhat frightened.

When he went to see her in the afternoon, she would be charming, easy to get on with. Perhaps she spoke a bit too much about the great days of her family and of her gilded childhood.

Nevertheless she looked upon humanity with an amused

kindliness, except for the two creatures who assumed in her mind the quality of traitors in a melodrama, the two Sallenaves, father and son.

They had grown rich with the fortune that should have gone to her. Raoul Sallenave lived in a big apartment on Boulevard Raspail, and he had built a luxurious villa on the Seine, near the forest of Fontainebleau.

The Doise Biscuits! The Doise money! The Doise honesty, which had forced them to sell one of the rows of houses on the square which bore their name!

There was already talk at the period of demolishing everything in order to put up apartment houses, and Marguerite had received offers.

"Of course, I refused. I'd rather go without bread . . ."

He should have been wary. He listened with a smile. She asked him few questions about himself, and that should have alerted him.

In short, the only living creature that interested her was herself. She was part of the procession of her dead family which continued to surround her with a kind of protecting halo.

He now understood. She did not want a servant or a cleaning woman because she would not have been able to put up with a person of her own sex in the house.

Yet she needed help. She might need it. An illness, a broken leg, would be sufficient. She did not even have a telephone to call for help, for she had had the line disconnected.

"No one has any reason to telephone me. I'd jump with fright every time someone got a wrong number."

He had suspected her of avarice. And he was now sure that she was miserly and that avarice had played a role in their marriage: she would have someone at her disposal day and night without having to pay.

Bouin had a pension. He had once mentioned, casually, that in the event he remarried his widow would continue to receive two thirds of it.

As for her, she never spoke of what she owned. One side of the alley continued to belong to her. Once every quarter the tenants came to pay their rent. Each entered the dining room in turn. Bouin did not know what they paid, just as he did not know what his wife did with the money.

Did she deposit it in a bank? Did someone take care of investing it for her?

She alluded only to expenses, to repairs that were requested of her, to the roofs that leaked, to windows and doors that needed to be fixed.

"You'd think that they damaged things out of spite. The rents aren't enough for the upkeep of the houses."

She felt no affection for him. She had proved it when she had remained stiff and frigid in his arms. For her, he was a kind of servant.

Had he gone too far? Perhaps. He had a right to go far after what she had just done to him. He also had a right to drink. And to smoke his cigars.

What happened when he lit one in the living room after dinner, in front of the television set? She would open the window wide and cover herself with her heaviest shawl, which did not keep her from shivering so as to get across to him that she was risking pneumonia because of him.

That was just one detail. There were a hundred others. There were a thousand. For example, after they got married, he had suggested that they share household expenses. As he saw it, it was a matter of each one's paying a monthly sum to be fixed by mutual agreement.

However, after doing the marketing, she would take all the shopkeepers' slips and classify them in a drawer with the bills for electricity, water, sewage, and garbage collection.

He had been surprised, at the end of the first month, when she had declared: "I've done our accounts."

With her glasses on her nose, she had demanded that he check with her the bills of the shopkeepers, the laundry, etc.

"Check the addition. . . . Yes, I insist!"

She had divided the sum in half.

"We'll do the same thing every month. That'll avoid any arguments."

He had gone to get his money in the bedroom. He kept it in a drawer of the chest. He did not have the key to it and was not concerned about it.

What was the meaning of doing things this way? Was it love, was it affection, confidence?

When they went to the movies, each paid for his own ticket.

"It's fairer that way."

She would observe him when he ate, assuming a look of disgust when, for example, he would use a matchstick as a toothpick. By seemingly trivial words and by meaningful looks, she would underscore each of his bad manners.

Everything about him shocked her. It was not only the cat that slept against his legs every night.

"My first husband's skin was as smooth as a woman's," she once remarked when he was walking bare-chested in the bedroom.

That amounted to saying that the dark thick hair with which he was covered repelled her.

"She has always detested me."

The way she detested the Sallenaves. Perhaps out of a need to detest someone. Perhaps to fill her empty days.

He felt her always watching him from behind, furtively.

"Well! You've had something besides wine to drink today. . . ."

She was not mistaken. He had met an old friend and they had had two or three apéritifs.

She knew everything. She wanted to know everything. She took her time before asking seemingly innocent questions. None of them was really innocent. Some of them had to do with events that were several months in the past and about which she remembered everything.

She would compare the answers with others that he had given.

"But you told me . . ."

At times he felt as if he were at school, facing the teacher who was trying to pin a fault on him and who wasn't satisfied until he blushed before confessing.

"Is it true that your first wife wasn't jealous?"

"That's right."

"Then she didn't love you."

"I think she did. . . . We got on very well."

"Were you happy with her?"

"I didn't feel unhappy."

Angèle did not ask questions. There were no rules between her and him. They did not eat at a definite hour. If dinner was not ready, they would go to a restaurant.

Their rare disputes were rather part of a game.

"Did you take advantage of it?"

"Of what?"

"Of her not being jealous."

"Sometimes I did."

"And now?"

"So far I haven't."

He was lying. She could feel it. She had actual feelers.

"But you hope you will?"

"I hope nothing. I don't plan ahead."

"Your first wife wasn't very proud."

"Why?"

"Don't you understand?"

"No."

"To see one's husband come home after having just dirtied himself in the belly of another woman, of a woman he hardly knows and who perhaps has given him a nasty disease. To sleep in the same room as he, to share a bathroom . . ."

He found nothing to answer and would look at her with stupefaction.

"I wouldn't stand for it. . . . I'd say to him, 'You'd better leave.' "

As if talking to a servant!

Did Marguerite ever follow him in the street when he went out in the afternoon? He had suspected her of doing so. There were times when he turned around suddenly. He had, to be sure, seen her twice in the course of several months, the first time entering a store, the second time suddenly turning about. He had not questioned her when he got home.

He preferred not to think of those more or less disagreeable things in order to retain some pleasure in life.

Too bad for her if she was going to start spoiling things between them. He managed to fill his days with little pleasures, and he always had Joseph as a faithful companion, Joseph who sometimes seemed to reproach him for having changed houses, for having imposed a foreign presence upon him, in short, for having betrayed him.

Did she dare to beat the cat in his absence? He doubted it, because she was too afraid of it.

She had done better. She had killed it. And it was not only Joseph that she had thereby attacked, it was he himself, Emile, whose presence and smells she no more liked than she did those of the animal.

She had waited for the opportunity for years. She had not had the patience to wait longer, a year, perhaps two, until the cat died a natural death.

Bouin drank, but he felt cool and collected. He was convinced that he saw things more clearly, more objectively than ever.

She was a bitch. One had only to look at the photographs and see the awkward bearing of her first husband, the famous first violinist of the opera, to know that he was a weakling who had let himself be led by the nose for more than thirty years.

As for her father, Sebastian, that bloated half-wit, decked out with a charm-studded watch chain, he was so much in need of forgiveness for his many sins that he let his daughter get away with anything whenever he was home.

A bitch already when she went driving in the Bois de Boulogne in a carriage drawn by two horses. A bitch the day she married Frédéric Charmois. For there was, naturally, a wedding photograph too. The album was overflowing with photos. The biscuit factory seen from the street. The yard of the biscuit plant with the entire staff lined up in rows around Sebastian Doise.

Old Arthur Doise, in his armchair. The same in his office. His sister, with a hair-do like that of the Empress Eugénie. Other Doises, particularly old ones, a few babies on bear-skins, finally Marguerite, photographed by her fiancé on a riverbank, with her big hat and her parasol with the pointed tip.

The album sat in state on the piano, like a treasure.

Bouin did not have access to it. She had never asked him for a picture of himself. When they were married, she had not suggested that they be photographed.

Only one dog in the lot, a sleek, pedigreed animal, as distinguished-looking as the violinist husband.

No other animals. There was no place for animals, except for the parrot that Marguerite had bought a few weeks after Charmois's death, to replace him.

A parrot that did not talk. Wasn't that better? Did Charmois talk? He gave violin lessons. In the evening, he put on his dress clothes and white tie and took the subway at Denfert-Rochereau for the opera, where he proudly walked in by the stage door.

"God damn it to hell!"

He was in a fury. He felt unhappy. She had touched him in a sensitive spot, and he found no way of retaliating.

He hated her. Despised her.

"A bitch, that's what she is. . . ."

He missed Angèle, he felt like weeping over Angèle, talking to her, being comforted by her.

Angèle was a woman, a real one, a female, who did not come from sickening biscuits. Even the Doise biscuits were a bad memory, especially those that were baptized French Kisses. Pretentious and saccharine drivel typical of the family's mentality.

Actually, the plant manufactured cheap stuff, the kind of sweets that one doesn't buy for oneself but that one gives to children when one goes visiting and doesn't know what else to give them.

The French Kisses were made of cheap dough. One got the impression that one was eating sand. But they were sugar-coated in various colors and decorated with floral and arabesque designs.

When he was four or five years old, an old neighbor used to call him when he was playing in the street.

"Come here, child . . . I've got something good for you."

She would get her box of biscuits, Doise biscuits, and open it as if it were a jewel case. She would say to him, expecting to delight him, "Take one."

She lived alone. The neighbors thought her a bit mad.

They said that she had been an actress. She was the only one on the street who used make-up, and he was almost afraid of her coal-black eyes.

"The bitch . . ."

He was not drunk. She did not dare come down. From time to time he heard light footsteps above his head. Devious footsteps. Everything about her was devious.

"Do you want to go out, Emile? It's time for Coco's exercise."

For, of course, the parrot's name was Coco. It was stupid. It was bad-tempered. Like its mistress, it did not forgive Bouin for having invaded the house, and particularly for having brought with him an odd animal.

He was brooding over his grievances. The wine helped him. As one refills a stove, he kept finding grievances to add, and suddenly he stood up, bent on showing her who he was.

Did he have a definite aim when he entered the living room hesitantly?

He began by raising the blind, which had not yet been touched that morning. The snow was beginning to melt. There were still patches of it on the sidewalks on both sides of the alley. A little boy tried to slide on it, and Bouin was surprised to discover that outside life continued as on other days.

A sewer man, who was standing near a round hole, was beating his arms in order to get warm. He caught sight of Bouin behind the curtain and must have envied him, as though he himself would not reach the age of sixty-five, and be able to retire. And what of it? What would he do with himself?

Was Marguerite finally going to come downstairs? She had heard the sound of the blind. He imagined her with her ear glued to the door of the bedroom. She was wary of everything, particularly of him.

The parrot, in its cage, let out one of its piercing screams, and Bouin turned around with a hard and evil look on his face.

Now it was his turn to be vicious. She who always spoke about justice must have been expecting it.

Staring at the bird, which stared back at him, he strode over to the cage. He opened it and extended one arm prudently. The wings unfolded. He managed to grab one of them, while the bird sharply pecked at one of his fingers, drawing blood.

It was impossible to remove the bird by force through the narrow opening. He might have strangled it. He had just grabbed it by the neck, but that was not what he wanted. Putting his other hand into the cage, he pulled out a feather from the tail, the longest feather, a bright red one. He had to pull hard. He hadn't thought that the feathers were so firmly planted in the flesh. He pulled out two, three, four . . .

"You'll see a thing or two, old girl."

Five . . .

It was as if he were pulling out the feathers of the Doises.

Six . . .

Smaller and lighter feathers were coming out by the handful. Blood was flowing, from his hand and from the bird's behind.

He finally stopped, exhausted, slammed shut the cage, and, bending over, picked up the feathers from the floor.

He was nauseated and exhausted. He had no other desire than to go back to bed and sleep.

He looked at the multicolored feathers in his hands. They formed a kind of bouquet. In a vase, on the piano, there had always been a bouquet of strawflowers.

He removed the flowers and replaced them by the feathers, and he could not refrain from smiling slyly.

When he got to the entrance door, he opened it and threw the strawflowers on the powdery snow, where they scattered.

He and she met on the stairs. She must have seen the blood flowing from his hand, and she rushed to the living room. She uttered only one cry. He had reached the top of the stairs. He turned around, but even though there was a soft thud, it did not occur to him to go down again.

IV

It was not his fault. Marguerite was so aware of it that when he tossed a note into her lap reminding her of the cat's death, she dared not reply:

THE PARROT.

He felt sick, feverish. Because of the blow she had just dealt him, he had drunk more than usual, and he lived the last half hour in a nightmarish fog.

He remained standing a moment longer, tottering in front of the open door of the bedroom. His wife's bed was made. The room was tidy. His own bed was ready to receive him with fresh sheets and a clean pillowcase.

Wasn't that still another way of showing him that she was

a perfect wife, that she knew her duties, that all the wrongs were on his side, and that she was the victim?

The proof was that she was taking care of him despite his cruelty, that the evening before she had suggested that she apply mustard plasters, that she was worried about his comfort, that she changed the sheets of his bed even though it wasn't the day for it.

Was she still on the floor of the living room, in a faint, or pretending to be? She was hoping that he would get worried, that he would come downstairs, would get panicky, beg her pardon, perhaps send for a doctor.

He hesitated and finally, with a stony face, went to his bed, though he left the door open.

He kept listening. The fever took him back a long way in time, to the days when he was a child and had a sore throat or a bad cold. His sensations, his thoughts, which were sometimes vague and sometimes very precise, and the images that resembled dream-images, had a somewhat childlike quality, and hadn't he just behaved like a furious child downstairs?

It had relieved him for a moment. Had he really been relieved? Had he not forced himself to go to the very limit of his impulse, of the diabolical idea that had suddenly occurred to him?

He felt ashamed. He did not admit it to himself. Above all, he did not want to feel guilty toward her. What he would have liked, as when he was little, was a good sickness, a real one, that would endanger his life and oblige the doctor to come to see him two or three times a day.

Marguerite would be frightened, in spite of everything.

She would be torn by conflicting feelings, and she would finally recognize that she was wrong and would be ashamed, instead of him.

He would not be sick. He would have to make do with a hang-over. Coughing, wiping his nose, sweating in bed without anyone's pitying him.

Nobody had the right to claim that he was asking for pity. He didn't like to be pitied. He was a man and had always been self-sufficient.

Was it absolutely true?

He was faking, was rejecting thoughts that were not yet formed and that by taking shape might become unpleasant. He kept listening. He still hesitated about getting up and going downstairs.

"You're beginning to realize that this time it doesn't work, old girl."

It was funny. At times, he confused Marguerite with his mother.

She was moving about below. He caught the slightest noise, the slightest rustle of cloth. She was probably getting up slowly, she too listening intently. Then she stood up, and she probably looked at the cage and the plucked bird, for he could hear her sobbing. Between her sobs she stammered words that he could not make out, and then she walked to the hallway.

At the right was a bamboo coat hanger that must have been there in the time of Sebastian Doise. The leather vest was hung on it, and on the other side an old gray coat of Marguerite's.

She must have slipped it on and put her rubbers on over

her shoes. The street door opened and shut, and he could hear footsteps on the sidewalk.

He ran to the window and saw her walking hurriedly toward Rue de la Santé. Her hands were empty. He could sense that she was agitated, and, though she was not gesticulating, she was probably still mouthing her dramatic monologue.

Where was she going? He wondered for a moment whether she was not on her way to the police station to complain about what he had done, but as soon as he got back to bed he fell asleep.

He continued to be conscious of the situation. Something very serious had happened. The rest of his life might very well be changed as a result. Nothing enabled him to foresee exactly what would happen.

So what! Much better that way! It was bound to happen one day or other, something was bound to explode. He had put up with the old woman's sneaky attacks long enough.

For, though he did not feel old, he saw her as old. Older than his mother, since the latter had died at fifty-eight.

She would find a way of having the last word. Who knows if she had not got it into her head to go to see a lawyer.

A half hour went by, and he started every time he heard a sound in the alley.

All her life, Marguerite had foreseen misfortunes from which she suffered in advance, even though they never took place. Her avarice, for example. She had a sickly fear of the future, and she remembered her father's ruin, the business falling into the hands of strangers.

She might fall sick, find herself suddenly immobilized forever. If she had counted on him to look after her, she no longer did. She would need a nurse. Would she be able to pay for one for years?

The word "hospital" haunted her. She was seized with panic at the thought of finding herself at the mercy of everyone, in an unknown bed and surrounded by the curious eyes of eight or ten sick persons.

She needed money, if only to pay for a stay in a private clinic.

She had already thought of the matter when Frédéric Charmois was still alive, perhaps during her father's lifetime too.

She was afraid of everything, of the wind and the thunder, and above all of poverty.

"She'll bury me. . . ."

He had often thought that. He had said it to her. She had once murmured:

"I hope so."

She had added:

"It's less painful for a woman to remain alone than for a man. . . . Men are unable to look after themselves. . . . They're softer than we are."

She always finished by being right. The proof was that whereas she was bravely walking in the cold and snow to go God knows where, he remained wallowing in his bed, groaning and disgusted with himself.

Footsteps . . . Footsteps of two persons . . . One of them was a man. . . . The key entered the lock. . . .

"Come in, Doctor."

He did not understand why she had brought back a

doctor, unless it was not for herself but for him. And what if she had gone for an alienist with the thought of having him committed?

They entered the living room, the door of which then shut, and Bouin could hear only a hushed murmur. It went on a long time. He tried in vain to understand. After all, the man she had called doctor must have been a veterinarian.

That was it. She had gone for a veterinarian to treat the parrot. He was not mistaken. The living-room door finally opened and then the street door, and when he rushed to the window, he saw a man, from the back, carrying off the cage, which was covered with the flannel cloth that was used at night.

He got into bed again, waited awhile, and finally fell asleep.

Later, he heard familiar sounds, very far off, in another world. He recognized the old woman's step on the floor of the bedroom, and there was the shock of a plate or a cup against the marble of the night table.

He did not open his eyes. The footsteps moved off. She went down the stairs. He did not move, and he felt beads of sweat forming slowly on his forehead. It became a game. He tried to guess where the next drop was going to emerge. Sometimes it was near one of the temples, and sometimes in the middle of the forehead, and from time to time there was also one near the nostrils.

Opening his eyes, he saw the bowl, which was still steaming slightly. He was not hungry. He refused to touch the food that she had brought for him out of duty or pity.

Who knows whether she did not intend to get rid of him as she had got rid of the cat?

It was the first time that the idea occurred to him. The thought was still vague, and he did not really believe it. It was part of the fever, and the wine he had drunk had something to do with it.

"That would suit her. She would inherit the pension without having to put up with me any longer."

There was a contradiction in this which he preferred not to see. If she had married so as not to be alone and to be assured of free help in case of need, his disappearing would be of no advantage to her.

But was she thinking about what she was doing? Wasn't she steeped in hatred? A hatred that did not date from that morning, that had nothing to do with the parrot, but that went very far back. It was idiotic to say so, but perhaps it dated from before she knew him.

He remembered her cold, hard look when, after having hesitated for a long time, he had stretched out over her with the intention of making love. When, not without difficulty, he entered her, her whole body had suddenly stiffened as if it were instinctively repelling the male.

For perhaps a moment, he had hoped that she was going to relax, but she did not. He had withdrawn shamefully, muttering excuses.

"Why?" she asked in a toneless voice.

"Why am I apologizing?"

"Why don't you go on and why don't you have your fun? I married you. It's my duty to submit to that too."

The "too" had recurred to him many times. What exactly did it mean? What else was she submitting to out of a Christian sense of duty? His cigars? His uncouthness? The fact of sharing the same bedroom?

There were two empty bedrooms on the second floor. One served as a storage room and the other had been her room when she was a girl; she had kept it intact, with all the objects in place, and probably considered it as a kind of sanctuary.

She had shown it to him only once, from the threshold; he had not been asked to step in, and the door was always locked. She opened it only when he was not there, at least that's what he supposed.

She was in the kitchen. She was eating, in spite of her grief. He made an effort to overcome his dizziness and, resting on one elbow, he took the bowl that contained the now tepid vegetable soup.

He sniffed at it mistrustfully, put his lips to it, and found that the liquid had an odd taste.

Could it be that it was now he who was putting on an act? If she meant to poison him, she would not do it so soon after the death of the cat or after the incident of the parrot.

Nevertheless he got up and went, in his bare feet, to pour the contents of the bowl into the toilet, eating only the biscuit that was on the plate.

He was not hungry. He was not shaved, nor had he taken a shower, and he felt dirty.

It was a painful afternoon, the kind that one later tries to forget about. He slept, woke up several times, once when it was dark and the street lamp was lit in the alley.

He listened but heard nothing. For more than a quarter of an hour, he lay there on the watch, and he became aware of his loneliness. He felt that Marguerite was not in the house. He was left to himself, and he was filled with anxiety.

Finally he made up his mind to go downstairs, which he did on tiptoe. There was no light in the living room, no fire on the hearth. It was very cold. The absence of the cage left a void, and the room seemed larger, the piano enormous.

The dining room was not lighted either, nor was the kitchen, but everything was tidy.

He drank another glass of wine, defiantly. He had no desire to drink. The wine seemed bitter to him. Then he went upstairs very quickly, afraid that his wife might find him on the ground floor.

He had never been so concerned with Marguerite's doings, which now assumed enormous importance.

He dozed off once again, but nevertheless heard her come in. They were both used to the noises of the house, of the slightest displacement of air.

She did not light a fire in the living room. Perhaps there were no split logs in the cellar; the supply upstairs had been exhausted for three days.

She stayed in the kitchen. Later, she went upstairs and remained standing in front of him, watching him by the light of the hall lamp.

He pretended to be sleeping. She took away the cup and plate. He then had to go to the toilet, and he almost did not flush the bowl so as not to betray his presence there.

He slept again. She must have lain down, since, when he awoke in the middle of the night, he heard her regular breathing.

The next day was much the same. She went out twice, the first time to do the marketing and the second probably to go to the veterinarian's, the way one goes to see a sick person in a hospital.

Was Coco going to die? He hoped not, although he was frightened of the thought of their future encounters in the living room in the presence of the tailless bird.

He took advantage of his wife's being out to go downstairs and eat some bread. He felt worse that afternoon, and he vaguely saw her in front of him, with a blank look on her face and her eyes cold as when he had naïvely lain upon her.

"Do you want me to call the doctor?"

He shook his head.

"Do you need anything?"

He made the same movement. He was not putting on an act. He was very far away from her, in an incoherent world.

She went out again at about five o'clock, and he again went downstairs to eat something. His legs were weak. His head was spinning. He clung to the banister as if he were afraid of toppling forward.

He found a slice of ham in the refrigerator and ate it, holding it with his fingers. Then he ate a piece of cheese. It was Marguerite's dinner, but she could go and buy something else.

The following day, he knew it was Sunday because of

the silence. The universe was motionless. There was only the sound of church bells in the distance.

She had gone to mass. He no longer felt sick. He was very hungry. He felt a particular need to get rid of the smell of sweat and to shave.

He was weaker than he had expected, but all the same he took a shower. His hands trembled as he ran the razor over his cheeks. He sucked two eggs. In order to cook them, he would have had to use the frying pan or a pot, and he did not have the heart to wash them afterward.

What was it going to be like between Marguerite and him now that he no longer had any reason for staying in bed?

Wearing a pair of clean pajamas and his bathrobe, he went down to the cellar, split some logs, and carried them to the living room, where he lit a fire. As if to inform his wife that he was up and about, he opened the blinds. She would thus be warned before entering the house, which would give her time to compose herself.

It was for her to choose, not him. The house belonged to her. Most of the furniture was hers. Many of the objects were in the same place where they had been when she was born. Frédéric Charmois, even though he had lived there more than thirty years, had merely passed through and had left few traces, only some photographs and a violin in a locked closet.

Bouin could have gone off while Marguerite was away. A wheelbarrow would have been enough for him to remove his things. He had thought of doing so. He would think of it again when he was steadier on his feet.

He was anxious. The minutes and seconds were slow. The key fumbled before entering the lock and making the familiar click. If, in a period of a few years, he had so accustomed himself to the sounds and smells of the house, to the very quivering of the air, what effect would the slightest change have on Marguerite, who had lived there the seventy-one years of her existence?

She entered the dining room where they had never had a meal but where a family had formerly gathered around the oval table beneath the kerosene chandelier, which had been successively transformed for lighting by gas and then electricity.

She was in the kitchen. She did not stay there long, but she had opened the refrigerator and therefore knew that he had eaten two eggs.

She went upstairs and entered the bedroom which had been hers when she was a girl. He was impatient, resented her keeping him on tenterhooks. Wasn't she doing it on purpose, in order to punish him?

The bedroom was decorated with flowered cretonne. In a corner was a little writing desk on which, fifty-five years before, she had perhaps confided her girlish thoughts and feelings to a diary.

If he had known her at that time . . . But he was then only a rough-mannered mason's apprentice at whom she would not have deigned to look.

The door of a car slammed. It was the engineer, who had started his engine going and then had gone to get his family. At that time of year they did not go to the country.

Probably they would be spending the Sunday at the home of the parents of one or the other or of a sister or brother in the suburbs or elsewhere.

Everyone lived in a more or less limited circle. His and Marguerite's circle was limited to the walls of the house.

He had never had that impression with Angèle, perhaps because they almost never stayed at home, except for occasional meals, for making love, and for sleeping.

Yet they had few friends. They went anywhere and drifted with the crowd, where they did not feel lonely.

Had Bouin felt alone when he lived opposite, and had only a room and a bathroom? He never thought about it. He was neither sad nor melancholy, and he never had the agonizing impression of moving about in the void.

Here he sometimes wondered whether the objects, the furniture and knickknacks, were real. Everything was in its place, immutably, for eternity.

When Marguerite watched television, he would sometimes notice her profile, and she too was so frozen that he was surprised to hear her breathe.

It was she who had wanted him, out of fear of that immobility, of that silence. When they had both sat down in the kitchen to drink a glass of her sickening liqueur, she had suddenly realized that something was changed, that a quiver of life had entered the house.

In order to make the man stay, to be able to live as a couple without sin, she had had to marry him.

An old faded couple. Did the people who saw them, the neighbors and shopkeepers, find them pitiful or grotesque?

What would they have thought if they had observed them both in the house?

A door shut. Footsteps. Another door. He waited for her to come downstairs. She reached the hallway and hesitated.

Finally, stiff and inexpressive, she came into the living room. She faced him. Their gazes met, without warmth, without possible contact. With thin, trembling fingers, she handed him a piece of paper.

He stood there for a moment without reading what was written on it and finally glanced at it while she moved toward her armchair. Before sitting down, she picked up the knitting that was on the seat. He read:

I HAVE THOUGHT IT OVER. AS A CATHOLIC, I AM NOT ALLOWED TO DIVORCE. GOD HAS MADE US HUSBAND AND WIFE AND WE MUST LIVE UNDER THE SAME ROOF. HOWEVER, I AM NOT OBLIGED TO SPEAK TO YOU AND I REQUEST THAT YOU NOT SPEAK TO ME.

She had signed the note, with the angular, regular penmanship that she had learned from the nuns: "Marguerite Bouin."

The game had just begun.

The next day, for the first time since he had lived in the house, he made his bed, while she was making hers.

He was not trying to provoke her. He was no longer sick. His mind was clear. Since they no longer spoke to each other, since there were no further bonds between them, except for their signature on a register, it was natural to accept nothing from her.

It was perhaps childish, but he was determined about it, and when he saw her getting ready to go out to do the marketing he wrote on a slip of paper:

I'LL EAT OUT.

He was being strictly honorable in not having her cook for two, for he had decided not to eat anything that she prepared.

He took his meal at a small restaurant in the neighborhood and did not speak to anyone, and he avoided going to the café where he would have met people whom he knew.

Without admitting it to himself, he was in a hurry to get home, to know what she was doing. When he got to the house there was no one there, and he did not know what to do. It was confusing. On other days, he never wondered how to occupy himself.

It was three in the afternoon. He opened the refrigerator to try to see what she had eaten. He found a bit of paté, two potatoes separately wrapped, and some string beans in a bowl.

The two preceding days, she had left later. Did that mean that today she was going somewhere else?

He was worrying for no reason. He went up to the bedroom floor, opened the wardrobe, and saw that she had not taken her woolen coat but the fur coat that as a rule she wore only on Sunday.

He would not be able to question her when she got back and would have to be satisfied with observing and trying to guess.

Was the parrot dead?

He was annoyed with himself, though he was never going to admit it. Did she regret having poisoned his cat?

He lit the fire and was reading his paper when she returned. She went to the upper floor and then down to the kitchen. She made only a brief appearance in the living room to get her knitting.

Was she going to install herself in the dining room or the kitchen, where it wasn't warm enough?

Empty hours, without color, without light or shade, with only the kind of thoughts that one isn't proud of, futile, if not ridiculous, questionings.

"Who knows if she's not going to try to poison me?"

And he suddenly wondered:

"Would I be sad if she died?"

No! Not sad. Not unhappy. Perhaps he would miss her. He did not like people to die. It was not because he liked them, but rather because he dreaded death.

At their age, what chance did either of them have of living much longer?

Sometimes, when he lay in bed, he crossed his hands on his stomach, and if he noticed it before falling asleep he hastily changed his position, for the other was too reminiscent of a corpse in a funeral chapel.

Where would the mortuary chapel be set up? In the bedroom? In the living room? He imagined it in detail, the arrival of the coffin that smelled of freshly sawed wood.

He did not want to die first. Nor did he want her to die. He had to think of something else. He preferred to go off, to walk in the streets, despite the cold and the wind. For the wind had succeeded the snow and was driving the clouds across the sky.

He had not dared drink his glass of wine in the kitchen, where Marguerite was. He was not far from Nelly's place. He decided to go over, without any definite intention. It was not like the other times.

He had known Nelly a long time, more than ten years, almost fifteen. He already frequented her little café on Rue des Feuillantines during the lifetime of her husband, Théo, as everyone called him.

You went down a blue stone step. The floor was paved with red tiles on which sawdust was sprinkled.

The bar was at the back, near the glass door of the kitchen that was covered with a thin curtain.

When Théo was still alive, there were first and foremost the regulars, at all hours of the day. In the morning it was mainly workmen, who drank coffee or white wine before going back on the job. Later came the shopkeepers and artisans of the neighborhood, who appreciated the Loire wines and Théo's good humor.

The color of his face was almost as glowing as that of the tiles. His main activity was to disappear by the trap door behind the counter at about ten o'clock and bottle the wine in the cellar.

His wife took his place and stood right above the trap door.

"That way, you're sure he won't escape," the customers would say jokingly.

Nelly was a juicy girl, twenty years younger than Théo.

Bouin was not the only one to take advantage of her temperament.

She was always ready to make love, which she did as naturally as the clients drank their glass of wine. Once when Emile asked her whether she never wore panties, she replied, banteringly but sincerely:

"And run the risk of missing an opportunity?"

It is true that Théo's almost continuous presence, the fact that the café was open to everyone, and the topography of the place made amorous exercises rather difficult and brief.

Early in the morning, at about eight o'clock, it was still easy, because then Théo was doing his marketing in the neighborhood. A look at Nelly as she leaned idly on the bar was sufficient for her to understand. She would answer likewise with a look. It was either yes or no. Almost always yes.

After a brief moment, she would head for the kitchen, where Bouin would follow her. With the door closed, she could see through the curtain whether anyone entered the café, while she herself remained invisible.

It had to be done standing up, always in the same place. She would lift up her skirt with a gesture that was so natural that it was not indecent, and she would offer a white, fleshy rump.

Did she really get to enjoy herself too, or did she only pretend? He had asked himself the question without being able to answer it. It was possible that if she was always ready it was because she never quite made it.

If a customer or even Théo arrived, the maneuver was

easy. One simply left by the second door, which led to the hallway of the building, and went directly to the street.

She must have aged since the first time he had ventured to court her, but, as he had aged along with her, he hardly noticed it.

"A glass of Sancerre."

"A big one?"

She had emerged in blue house slippers from the depths of the kitchen where she had put a pot on the fire. She ran a hand through her hair, which fell over her cheeks as always.

"I thought you were dead."

It was hardly the moment to utter that word, when he was living with the thought of death, that of Joseph, perhaps the parrot's, who knows, his own one day or other.

"Is it true that you've remarried?"

Her lips parted over her fine teeth, and her eyes were moist. Leaning on the bar, with her chin on her hands, she offered Bouin a view of her white breasts.

He had always known her dressed in black. One might have thought that she wore the same dress over the years.

"It's true."

"It seems you've made a fine marriage, a rich wife, who has a street of her own."

He did not like that subject of conversation and emptied his glass.

"Let me have another. . . . Will you have something?"

"A small cassis."

They did not quite know what to say to each other. He wondered whether he was going to give the usual signal.

"It's not the small old lady dressed in magenta I saw you with last fall on Rue Saint-Jacques?"

It must have been a fine sunny day, for Marguerite's magenta suit was rather light, and she usually wore it with a white hat.

"Life moves on. Too bad we don't see you more often. . . . Have you retired?"

"I retired some time ago. . . ."

"Things are quiet here. . . . The old-timers are dropping out one after the other. . . . The young ones don't appreciate places like this. . . . They think they're old-fashioned, and they're not far out. . . . There are days when I wonder whether I'm not going to put the key under the door and wind up my days in the country."

How old could she be? As far as he could tell, she had been about thirty when he had followed her into the kitchen for the first time. Théo had died of a stroke seven years ago. She must be around forty-five, and her face was still smooth.

When she became a widow, her behavior in no way changed.

She was free. She no longer had to account for herself to anyone. Yet she had never invited him to go up to her bedroom. He had never seen her entirely naked, and their relationship had remained rather furtive.

She belonged to everyone, almost like a woman of the streets. Nevertheless, she felt the need to have a personal domain, a place to which nobody was admitted.

"You've become thin."

"A little, yes."

"Aren't you well?"

"I've just had the flu."

"Troubles? Things not going well with your wife?"

"Oh, it's all right."

She looked at him as if she were reading his mind. Her cat looked at him in exactly the same way.

"Oh, forget it!" she exclaimed, as if in conclusion to confidences which he had not made.

And, straightening up, she gave him the signal, a wink, a barely perceptible movement of the head.

He dared not say no. On entering the café, he must have expected that that would happen. Wasn't that why he had come? Wasn't it a kind of test?

He followed her. She looked at him laughingly.

"Admit that you hesitated. . . . For a moment I thought you were going to refuse. . . . You didn't look very gay. . . . Let's see if you're still the same. . . ."

It amused her. Perhaps that was her entire secret. If she accepted men's caresses so easily, if she provoked them with calm immodesty, it was probably less out of sexual need than because they amused her.

"Fine! . . . That's better."

He had feared that he would not make it, and now he found himself in a familiar womb, as when he was fifteen years younger, as in the time of Angèle, before he married Marguerite.

A childish thought occurred to him. He would have liked his wife to loom up, to see him as he was at that moment. It was of her that he was thinking, of the magenta suit that had just been mentioned, of her expressionless face of the day before and of that morning.

From here, the house in the alley became unreal. Marguerite too, and her ancestors the Doises, the man with the watch chain and the founder of the biscuits, the husband with the violin who left in evening clothes for the opera, the semidarkness in the rooms, the cheerless fire and the evenings passed in silence, in the darkness, in front of the television set.

He would have liked it to last a long time, so that he could remain in that state of mind.

"Are you keeping an eye on the door?" she asked, out of breath.

For it was up to him to be sure that nobody came in.

"I am. . . ."

He stood motionless for a moment, catching his breath, while Nelly let her skirt down.

It was over. All that remained was a kitchen that was not much lighter than their house, a smell of leeks mixed with that of armpits and the whiffs of wine that impregnated the whole building.

"Satisfied?"

"Thanks."

He said it sincerely. He would have liked to express his gratitude to her. She had given him pleasure so often, without asking for anything, without expecting anything in return.

Others who had taken advantage of her as he did must have spoken of her as a whore once they were with their friends.

Emile had a feeling of gratitude and warmth toward her. He would have liked to talk with her, to have gone up to her bedroom, to have shared a real intimacy with her.

When he became a widower, he thought seriously about her several times, for Théo was already dead.

It annoyed him, of course, that so many men had been in the kitchen, like himself. He suspected that she would never become a faithful wife. But had Angèle been faithful to him? He did not know and preferred not to raise the question.

What he liked about Nelly was that she was real. He was fond of her. He now was sorry that he had waited so long before going to see her.

If he had come more regularly to the café perhaps he would not have let himself be taken in.

For he had let himself be taken in and had lost touch with the rest of the world. He rubbed shoulders with people in the street, but did not really see them. He no longer knew what a woman was, or a child, laughter or tears.

He lived in a ghostly world that was both precise and inconsistent. He knew every flower on the wallpaper in the living room, the spots that had been made in Charmois's time, the photographs, the steps of the stairway that creaked, and the crack in the banister.

He knew the light at every hour of the day, in every season of the year, and Marguerite's face, her thin figure, her even thinner lips, the too white and too delicate skin of her chest when she undressed for the night.

It was an obsession. He had let himself be locked in

and now he was a prisoner for life. He ought not to have burned the note. The text of it was eloquent. She regarded him as her property and, in the name of religion, did not allow him to regain his freedom.

"What are you thinking about?"

He tried to smile.

"Nothing definite."

"All the same, you're not the kind who's sad after making love."

It was nice of her to say that.

"Lots of men are ashamed and don't dare to look at you. Are there women like that too?"

He almost replied that he knew at least one who was ashamed even before beginning.

In general, Nelly was right. He searched among his memories.

"Maybe we're more realistic," she said.

Two customers came in, metalworkers or typographers, judging from their gray smocks.

"Two small white wines."

They waved a greeting, glanced at Emile, then continued with their conversation.

". . . So I said to him, straight to his face: If that's the kind of customer you are, you can repair it yourself. Can you beat it? Twenty francs for a job that would have taken me more than three hours!"

Nelly winked at him, and, since the café was dim, stretched out her arm to turn on the light.

"Your health, Justin."

"Yours."

They must have been around sixty. They did not yet realize the speed at which they were going to age.

"How much do I owe you?"

"Three Sancerres and one glass of white wine . . . For you, it comes to two francs and eighty centimes. . . . Actually, it would be the same price for anyone else."

He was in the street again. There were the wind, the lights, the displays, the smells of the stores. There were also men, women, children being dragged by the hand, infants pushed in carriages. They had always been there. They would always be there. Life flowed around him, but he did not have the sensation of flowing with it.

He had become a stranger. Marguerite had become one before him, and who knows, perhaps she had always been a stranger.

That little girl who looked as if she had stepped out of a bandbox, whose photograph he had gazed at, wasn't she already outside the world?

As one looked at the photograph, one felt like shaking her, waking her up, saying to her:

"Look!"

Look and feel! Touch! The trees, the animals, the men . . . There's the sun. . . . A fine, useful rain is falling. . . . It's going to snow, it's snowing. . . . And now the wind is starting up. . . .

You're cold. . . . You're warm. . . . You're alive. . . . You're vibrating. . . .

He was walking mechanically, with his head down, without having to watch his way, like an old horse returning to the stable.

He turned the corner of the alley. Silence reigned. A few windows were lit, with a dismal yellow light. A house, then another one, all of them alike. The last one. The fountain in front of the end wall, and the naked little figure that held the spitting fish.

He took the key from his pocket, sniffled before opening, wiped his nose, and, while he was at it, wiped the wetness on his cheek.

V

For five days, he had eaten out, without pleasure. He would get up at 6:00 A.M., lock himself up in the bathroom, go downstairs, and prepare a cup of coffee or even drink his glass of red wine immediately.

In the silence and emptiness of the ground floor, he would then do his part of the household chores. He did his job very carefully, as if he feared a comment or reproach. It was becoming a kind of mania, and the piano had never shone so brightly.

His last job was to go down to the cellar, split wood, bring up a basketful, and light the fire in the living room.

Marguerite would come down at about half past eight, already fully dressed. Without seeming aware of the presence of a man around her, she would prepare her breakfast, then, putting on her everyday green coat, she would head for Rue Saint-Jacques.

He would sometimes follow her even if he did not need anything, simply for want of anything else to do. When she returned, she would put her purchases into the refrigerator and the cupboard, and she would go upstairs to tidy herself up and take her fur coat with her.

Twice a day, in the morning and the afternoon, she would go off to a mysterious appointment, probably with the veterinarian who was looking after her parrot.

Bouin did not know either his name or his address. He knew only, because he had seen him through the window when he was carrying off the cage, that the veterinarian was a short man with a limp and that he wore a tight overcoat.

He dared not go back to the café, perhaps because the pull was too strong. He was suspicious of the way he thought about Nelly and he realized the danger.

With her, he had no need to watch himself. He relaxed. The complications of the alley disappeared, lost their importance, or seemed absurd. If he let himself go, he would end by getting used to remaining there. It would become a weakness. He would drink his small glasses of wine and make use of Nelly when he felt like it.

He had no projects. Nothing was yet standard in the house. Each of them came and went, seeking his place, his rhythm, his schedule, somewhat the way the members of an orchestra tune up their instruments in the pit.

On the fourth or fifth day—he had stopped counting—

he followed his wife from a distance when she went to her afternoon appointment. It was already dark.

She went down the almost deserted Rue de la Santé, passed the prison and then the asylum. There were few people in the street, and one could hear their footsteps from a distance.

She then took Rue Dareau, which was hardly livelier, and finally arrived at Rue du Saint-Gothard, near the railroad.

She did not try to see whether she was being followed. She walked rather fast for a person of her age. She stopped in front of a curious building, which seemed to be an ancient farmhouse, with an inner yard beyond the gate. It was a rustic house, and there were other buildings that were as low as stables.

When she crossed the paved yard, dogs barked in these buildings. Then she went up a short flight of steps, rang a bell, and waited for the door to open.

After she had disappeared inside, he went up to the gate and read on an enamel plaque:

DR. PERRIN
VETERINARY CLINIC

She went there as one goes to see a patient in a hospital, and her visits indicated that the parrot was not dead.

He regretted what he had done, even after the poisoning of his cat. He would have liked to tell her so, but it was too late. Besides, he did not wish to give her the satisfaction of seeing him humiliating himself.

Did she too regret what she had done? No. She was not

the kind of woman to have regrets. She was always right. She was sure of herself. She took the right course. It was enough to see her look of assurance when, particularly on Sunday, she returned from church. Her clothes then smelled of incense. One would have thought that her eyes were clearer and purer, as if she had just caught a glimpse of the beatitudes of heaven and of eternal life.

He hated Sunday, the quietness of it, the lowered blinds of the shops, the people one met in the streets where they had nothing to do. They did not walk the way they did on weekdays. They were not going anywhere, or, if they did have a goal, they were not in a hurry.

They were bored too in their Sunday clothes and were afraid that their children would get themselves dirty. When he was young, quarrels broke out almost every Sunday between his father and mother, who were decent people all the same, used to knuckling under and to taking life as it came.

"Go for a walk."

He would go along the canal or along the Seine. They would give him a coin to buy ice cream in summer or candy in winter, and he always chose hard candies that lasted as long as possible.

Even on the barges, the families were as if frozen, and, toward the end of the afternoon, one was sure of meeting men who were drunk.

That Sunday he found his usual restaurant closed and had to go as far as Avenue du Général Leclerc for lunch. Later, he went by Nelly's café, the blinds of which were lowered too.

What did Nelly do on Sunday? She certainly didn't attend mass. She probably stayed in bed late, loitered about her bedroom, in the kitchen, in the dark little café where nobody came to bother her.

In the afternoon, perhaps she went to a movie. He had never seen her in the street. He knew her only in her black dress and her house slippers.

Marguerite had not gone to the clinic, which was also closed on Sunday. She did not go out in the afternoon, and they remained sitting in the living room in front of the television set watching a soccer game, a few songs, an animated cartoon. Finally a Western.

They were making time pass. She was knitting. Two or three times it seemed to him that her face was softening, that as she raised her head she was about to speak to him.

He pitied her a little. Since she was unable to make the first gesture, he was tempted to make it himself. He too opened his mouth, to say, for example:

"We're acting like children. . . ."

No. She would not accept that definition of their attitude.

"Listen, Marguerite, let's try to forget."

Nor that either. She was forgetting nothing. She remembered, with supporting dates, each disappointment, each offense since her childhood, each of her sorrows.

She needed to be unhappy, a victim of men's wickedness, and to forgive them with her lips.

"Poor woman . . ."

It was he who had been wrong. He ought not to have married her. What was it that had made him come back so many afternoons to the little house where she offered him a cup of coffee and, later, a glass of wine?

Was he not impressed by the fact that she was the owner of half of the street, the daughter of Sebastian Doise, a delicate creature, with a slightly faded elegance in her pastel-colored clothes?

He had not thought of money. Not crudely. Money nevertheless did appear as a kind of background of that row of houses that belonged to Marguerite, and the little figure with the fish took on a symbolic quality.

Bouin had just entered, almost by accident, a world which he had glimpsed only from a distance and to which it had not occurred to him that he would ever be admitted.

Was he really admitted? He had stopped a simple leak. The woman had offered him a glass of cordial, as to a workman who has finished a job in the house.

"Why not come back tomorrow for a cup of coffee?"

In the kitchen. It was only after two weeks that she had taken him into the living room.

The photos had impressed him, particularly that of the carriage drawn by two horses, and also the one which showed her walking by the water in her big straw hat.

He remembered his childhood when he had seen an elegant woman lift her skirt to enter a carriage or when, in the Bois de Boulogne—he had been there only two or three times, for it was far from home—he admired the women on horseback.

"Did your father have horses?"

"He could have had them. He preferred to hire a carriage by the day. I took riding lessons in an academy."

The horses in particular set him dreaming.

112

"Only in the academy?"

"We used to go riding in the Bois de Boulogne with the teacher."

In the beginning, she liked to talk about her life, jumping from one period to another.

"Twice a week my husband took me to the opera in the evening. I had a reserved seat."

She had kept the Liberty silk evening gown, embroidered with pearls, which she wore on those occasions and the white, elbow-length kid gloves.

"Don't come tomorrow. My tenants will be queuing up to pay the rent."

What could the seven houses that she still owned bring in? He had no idea, but the thought of her receiving people who came to pay tribute to her in the overheated living room was glamorous to him.

She had no need to do housework. She had told him so.

"I'd be bored if I did nothing, and if I got bored I'd get sick. I'd become like so many women of my age who think only of their little ailments."

He protested with a gesture.

"Tut, tut! I know what I'm saying. I'm not forgetting my birth date. But I swore to myself never to complain. It's when one starts coddling oneself that one gets old."

He and Angèle had also gone strolling on Sunday along the Marne, near Lagny. They would push each other for the fun of it and, when no one was around, they would take a roll in the tall grass. He remembered Angèle's smell, her laugh, for she often laughed when making love.

"Don't you think it's funny? I don't know who invented this business, but he deserves a statue."

When they kissed on Sundays, their saliva had a taste of the countryside.

Marguerite was dreamy and distant in the photograph. She looked so vulnerable that he would have liked to protect her.

At bottom, it was to some extent the photographs that he had married, the baby grand piano that gleamed in the semidarkness, the Louis Philippe and Second Empire furniture, the fountain in the alley, and the high smokestack on Rue de la Glacière.

He should have said no. He had been naïve and foolish enough not to understand, and he had made her unhappy.

"How about a movie?"

For he had tried to take her out.

"What's playing?"

"A Western."

"I hate fighting and shooting."

He would sometimes take her to a restaurant. She would look around suspiciously, would wipe the knife and fork, would sniff at the dishes before eating.

"It's cooked in margarine."

Or: "The waiter ought to wash his hands before serving."

She lived in a world of her own, an invisible world that she colored to suit her taste. And now she had to put up with a real man, a noisy man, with a heavy gait, who smoked foul cigars and emitted an animal smell.

To top it all, he had introduced into her carefully protected domain an animal that crept along the furniture the way a wild beast rubs itself against the bars of its cage and that stared at her but accepted familiarities only from its master, its god.

For Emile Bouin was a god to Joseph, and that annoyed her.

Bouin had sacrificed nothing for her, had not tried to integrate himself into her universe.

They had thus lived in their corner, each growing irritated with the other's gestures and intonations.

Had they not ended by taking a secret pleasure in their relationship? Children play at war. They were doing the same thing. But more passionately.

Each thought of the death of the other, each, in a more or less avowed way, wished for it, wished to be the survivor.

Marguerite had already got rid of her obvious enemy, of the cat whose mere presence was a defiance of the Doises and their sensitivity.

Why would she not get rid of her husband someday in the same way?

He had read in a paper that most acts of poisoning were committed by women. The article added that there were probably ten times as many cases as were discovered, for the family doctors, in the case of a sick or elderly person, signed the burial permits without investigating closely.

It was not yet fear, but he was beginning to be wary. He had another reason for not eating his wife's cooking. His decision to owe her nothing, to share in the household chores.

Since he made his bed, split the wood, lit the fire, waxed

the floor, and took out the garbage, why should he not also prepare his food, thus avoiding the necessity of going to the restaurant twice a day?

Just as he did not share Marguerite's bed, so he did not want to mix up his food with hers, and it did not displease him to surprise her and even to enrage her.

On Monday afternoon, he went to a furniture store on Boulevard Barbès.

"Don't you have one that locks?"

A cheap pinewood, white, lacquered kitchen cupboard with two doors.

"Locks can be put on for a slight additional cost."

"Good locks," he insisted. "Not the kind that can be opened with a hairpin."

The cupboard had been delivered on Thursday morning. That day, Marguerite had not gone out to visit the parrot, and she had cried part of the day. She was on edge, her eyes were red and her cheeks swollen.

She had watched with amazement as the huge yellow delivery truck with its large black lettering maneuvered before it was able to enter the alley.

She watched the delivery men who brought the cupboard into the kitchen and who asked:

"Where'll we put it?"

It was to her that they had put the question, and, without deigning to reply, she left the room.

"Here . . . To the right of the sink."

"Don't you think it's too big?"

It just about fitted into the space that Emile had intended for it.

That day he went on a buying spree, came back with canned goods, bottles of oil and vinegar, and all kinds of packages.

At noon, while his wife was upstairs, he had prepared his lunch, a huge beefsteak, browned potatoes, peas.

When she came down, she found him at the table, and she in turn prepared her snack.

The kitchen looked out on a yard six feet wide, on a blank gray wall. As they avoided looking at each other while eating, that was the only view they had. The sounds of the alley, of the city, did not reach them, except occasionally the distant zooming of a plane high in the sky.

The construction on the other side of the street had not begun. All they knew, from hearsay, was that certain tenants had been asked to leave. There was talk of building a school for nurses, others spoke of an office building, a modern garage, de-luxe apartments.

It was all the doing of the accursed Sallenaves, who had extorted half of the alley from a too credulous Sebastian Doise. With the money from the land, they were going to enlarge the new biscuit plant in Ivry.

A month went by. Marguerite received a letter that upset her. She dressed hastily and left the house rapidly. As he was not yet dressed to go out, he could not follow her.

He waited. They spent as much time waiting for each other as spying on each other, for they felt ill at ease when they were alone in the house. The absences of one partner or the other were like a kind of menace, especially if they occurred at unusual hours.

Where had Marguerite gone?

Where did Bouin go more and more often at about four in the afternoon?

They sometimes followed each other without concealing themselves, looking innocent, as it were.

Marguerite's return that day was as unexpected an event as the intrusion of the furniture truck in the alley. For the first time since he had known her, she came back in a taxi. The driver left his seat to help her remove the cage which they must have had difficulty getting into the car. Coco's cage, obviously.

He watched them from the living-room window. She insisted on carrying the cage herself, and she put it down carefully on the sidewalk, long enough to take out her key and open the door.

When she paid the fare, she uttered some words that Bouin could not hear, picked up the cage, which was covered with its flannel cloth, and a few moments later, without looking at her husband, set up the object in its usual place.

He remained near the window without moving, surprised and uneasy. He saw her remove the flannel and look tenderly at the parrot, which was standing on its perch.

It had all its feathers, and the tail was more brilliant than ever. Its protuberant eyes were staring straight ahead, and Bouin felt uncomfortable as in the presence of an incongruous spectacle. He suspected something unnatural. The bird did not move. Neither did Marguerite. She was communing inwardly, as if in the presence of the corpse of a beloved person.

He finally discovered the truth. The animal was dead.

It had been stuffed, its feathers had been replaced, and its eyes were made of glass.

After a while, Marguerite turned to him and looked at him sternly and defiantly.

Then she went to a small table on which were paper and a pencil. She wrote a few words, placed the sheet on the piano, and went to the hallway to remove her hat and coat.

Emile read:

IF YOU TOUCH IT, I'LL NOTIFY THE POLICE.

She did not return to the living room immediately, leaving him time to digest the warning. When she went back and sat down in her chair, not far from the parrot, he was sitting too, on the other side of the fireplace.

He wrote something on the page of a notebook, folded the paper very small, put it between his thumb and middle finger, and shot it into his wife's lap.

This time he missed.

He was to become more skillful later. The message struck Marguerite's knee and fell on the floor. She pretended to have seen and felt nothing. They remained motionless for a long time, as if in a state of suspended animation. Several times she looked at the parrot.

Finally, she let fall her ball of wool and, in picking it up, took the piece of paper, which bore a message for the first time:

THE CAT.

They were even.

His memory was not so good as in the past. He remembered events very well, remembered having been in such a place when it was raining or sunny, comments exchanged with the local shopkeepers, the huge lobster he had bought to astound Marguerite, the first mover's truck in the alley two houses below.

He remembered the text of his notes, of those that his wife, pursing her lips contemptuously, had left for him on the piano or night table.

But his memory was not reliable in the case of dates, in the sequence of facts. He had a tendency to telescope happenings, whereas they might have taken place over a period of two years. In order to establish the time, he was obliged to refer to the seasons, to the clothes that he and Marguerite wore.

The first moving, for example, had taken place during the first half of March, a month of March that was particularly radiant, for the newspapers quoted statistics and published photographs of the chestnut trees in bloom.

When all the windows were open in the alley, the latter was less dismal, less silent. A quiver of life ran through it, voices could be heard from one house to the next, or a child playing in the streets and called by its mother, a phonograph record, a radio, and the background noises of cars on Rue de la Santé and distant echoes from Carrefour Saint-Jacques.

Leaning at the window, he contemplated the furniture piled up in the moving van, thus discovering the tastes and a bit of the private life of people whom he had encountered only in the alley. He was surprised at the typewriter of a former officer, at a huge painting in a gilded frame representing a naval battle in the time of the buccaneers.

Marguerite also looked out from the second floor, but her window was closed, and she stood behind the curtain, without showing herself. She seemed to be suffering, she ate less than ever, and she began to show her age.

There were times when she did not put on make-up, whereas a discreet make-up had always given a certain freshness to her complexion. She seemed to have faded, grown gray, almost overnight.

She never entered the living room without first pausing for a moment in front of the parrot's cage, moving her lips as if in church.

Bouin could not get used to that silent presence. The dead parrot was more encumbering than the live one had been. In ceasing to move, it had taken on a mysterious and threatening expression, like that of certain African sculptures which he had seen in the window of a picture dealer.

There was no longer any need to cover the cage with the flannel cloth in the evening.

He hesitated to place the exact time of Madame Martin. Was it during the movings that had followed each other in the houses opposite? At that time, there were unusual comings and goings in the alley.

Men would arrive in cars, would move about with brief-cases under their arms, would consult plans, would stop, gesticulate, and then leave.

They were the architects and contractors and their technicians. After a moment, Marguerite would shut the windows so as not to see them.

He hoped at times that she would give in, would change her attitude, would turn toward him with a human look, with gentler eyes, and speak to him.

To say anything. For example, simply:

"It's time for lunch."

As elsewhere, in all houses, wherever human beings lived together.

He would have forgotten about the cat. Perhaps. Perhaps not for long. Especially as he had discovered other grievances.

At bottom, what he did not admit to himself was that he was afraid of her. She had more persistence than he, more energy, more self-mastery.

He would have been willing to go back to their old life, even if it meant quarreling after three days and returning to communication by notes.

But not she. Her face and gaze were as rigid as the parrot's body.

He pitied her. That tension was bound to become painful, and he was afraid that she might crack up.

He would immediately reply to himself: "Don't worry! A woman like that will never crack up. Not while you're alive. She wants your hide, and she knows that she'll finally get it. Until then, she'll hold out against everything."

It was in the summer. Around the month of August, for the butcher and the Italian grocer were on vacation, and they had to go a distance to find stores open. There were signs everywhere on the closed blinds of the shops, and they had to change laundries three times.

Bouin had got into the habit of following his wife when she did her marketing, although it was not yet a daily routine. On certain days he left the house first. On others, he went out later, around eleven o'clock, in order to have an apéritif on the way back.

He drank more than before, always red wine. It made him sleepy after meals, and he did not mind that drowsiness which gave him dreams that were closer to reality than his dreams at night. A foggy reality, voices, and postures that were slightly distorted.

He would remain seated in his armchair, with his head a bit heavy and his eyes half closed. For a while he would continue to see the shiny feet of the piano, the lions' paws in their glass supports. The image would gradually get cloudy and would be replaced by a tree in the Forest of Fontainebleau, and he would imagine that he was hearing the coarse, vulgar, but vivid voice of Angèle.

When they had brought her back from the hospital, after her accident, and he had bought her a lounge chair, for she could only take a few steps with crutches, he knew, as the doctor had told him, that she would remain crippled, but he was certain that she would live.

A year later, an ambulance took her to the hospital again, and for months he went to see her three times a week in a ward where other husbands sat like him and whispered at a bedside.

"Are you managing? It's not too bad?"

She acted gay.

"I have a good friend, the little redhead two beds away. Her name is Lili. She was a salesgirl . . ."

They gave her back to him six months later, without concealing the fact that her state was worse but that there was nothing more they could do for her. A neighborhood doctor looked after her. An old cleaning woman, Madame Blanquet, spent most of the day with her and prepared her meals.

Her legs swelled up. Then her stomach became enormous. The kidneys were affected. She had uremia. She did not know it, and she would call out to him while he was washing her:

"Say! You'd think I was pregnant."

One evening, a Friday, May 17th, he was in charge of a job near Porte de la Chapelle. Leo, the foreman, was an old friend.

"How about a drink?"

"My wife's waiting for me. You know she's laid up."

"A quick one!"

He had not lingered more than five minutes. When he got home, Madame Blanquet got up precipitately from her chair. Her eyes were red, and she watched him closely, as if she were afraid of a violent reaction on his part.

"I didn't leave her for a moment, I swear to you."

Angèle was dead. The old woman had closed her eyes. She seemed as enigmatic as Marguerite's parrot now did.

"When did it happen?"

"A half hour ago."

He had taken her hand, which was still soft, but had not been able to kiss her.

His mother had not even had a Madame Blanquet at her side when her time came. She was alone. He was already married. She had not been feeling well for some weeks, but continued to get up to look after the house.

He went to see her every evening, took her delicacies or

fruits. He had found her on the kitchen floor, with her eyes open.

He would sometimes be afraid of coming home and finding Marguerite dead in one of the rooms.

There was no resemblance among the three women, between his mother and Angèle, between the two of them and Marguerite, and yet, in his somnolence, they had a tendency to merge. Especially their voices, the words, the phrases they uttered. Perhaps a certain questioning in their looks.

Who knows whether the common element was in him rather than in them, a feeling of fear, as when he was a child and there was always something with which to reproach himself, an uneasiness, the sensation of being behind-hand, of not doing all that he should, of deserving to be scolded?

It didn't matter whether it was in June, July, or August. The period, in any case, when Marguerite was most edgy and could not sit still.

Two or three days went by without his following her when she went shopping. He felt a need for Nelly. He finally went to see her, and, as usual, he asked the silent question, received the signal, and followed her into the kitchen.

"You seem to have gone back to your old habits. Isn't your wife jealous?"

"We don't talk to each other."

"No kidding?"

"It's true."

"Wait . . . You're hurting me."

A long silence. He was out of breath. Then she continued, letting down her dress without losing the thread of the conversation:

"You mean to say that you both live in the same house without talking to each other?"

"I swear."

"And when you have something to say to each other?"

"We write notes."

"For example: I feel like making love."

"We've never made love."

"Doesn't she appeal to you? Or doesn't she want to?"

"Both. . . . I don't know. . . ."

He had felt a need to talk, and he was already annoyed with himself, as if the fact of mentioning Marguerite to Nelly were a fault, a lack of delicacy.

He stood at the bar, with a glass of Sancerre in his hand when, as he turned to the sunny street, he saw his wife on the sidewalk in the company of a woman about ten years younger than she whom he had already noticed with Marguerite. They were both walking slowly, as if to make the conversation last.

Was Marguerite likewise talking about him?

She was about to pass the café when she turned her head. She must have seen him, despite the semidarkness inside. She saw everything, sensed everything, especially when it had to do with him, particularly when it had to do with something he wanted to hide from her.

"Is that her?"

"Yes."

"Which of the two?"

"The older. The one in a pink dress."

"Does she always dress like that?"

"She wears only light colors, a little faded."

"She saw you."

"I think so too."

"Do you mind?"

"No."

"I'm not so sure. You're not going to be afraid to go back?"

"Afraid of what?"

"Tomorrow?"

"Probably."

"Here's to you."

But the next day he did not go to see Nelly. Something had happened in the house at the end of the alley. At about four o'clock, someone had rung at the door, which was rare. Without hurrying, Marguerite, who seemed to be expecting someone, had gone to open the door.

"How are you, Madame Martin?"

She was very dark, vigorous, with a man's shoulders and the shadow of a mustache.

"Am I disturbing you?"

Marguerite knew that Emile was in the living room, in his shirt sleeves, reading a magazine. In spite of it she brought in the visitor. He made as if to get up and greet her. Madame Martin hesitated and almost put out her hand, but she was already interfered with.

"Sit down here, please. It's the most comfortable chair, the one my mother seemed to prefer. I hardly knew her! Will you have a cup of tea? . . . Not now? . . ."

Madame Martin looked at him curiously, and he was embarrassed. Nevertheless, to leave the room would be to lose ground, and he remained where he was, pretending to read.

"I have very few callers, you know. I'm almost always alone. You're one of the rare people who visit me."

She added, following Madame Martin's gaze, "Don't pay any attention to him. I married him because I was sorry for him, I guess. He was a widower. He seemed unhappy. He lived right across the street in one of the houses they're going to tear down. I used to see him spend his days at his window.

"One day I invited him over for a cup of coffee, and he made a rather good impression. I realize now that he was intimidated. Intimidated and a hypocrite. For I've never known anyone as hypocritical as that man. Maybe it's not his fault. I discovered, too late, that he's not quite like other men. When he spoke to me, he was rude, so I asked him to be silent."

"Doesn't he speak to you any more?"

Just like Nelly a day earlier! Only Marguerite was being more cruel, more vicious than he had been on Rue des Feuillantines.

"For several months . . ."

"Not a word?"

"Not a word . . . Sometimes he rolls up a note and tosses it to me, and I don't even read it."

"Why?"

"Because I know in advance that it contains insults. The proof that he's not all there is that when his cat died, an old alley cat that he picked up somewhere or other, he accused me of having poisoned it. Me who had put up with its presence in the house and at night in our bedroom without saying a word. . . . It slept on its master's bed and kept me from sleeping with its snoring."

She looked at her husband severely, with a spark of triumph in her eyes. She had discovered a new way of taking revenge. The next day and the day after, Madame Martin would repeat the story in all the shops on Rue Saint-Jacques, and the shopkeepers would look at him with mingled pity and disapproval.

"Do you know what he did the day after?"

"The day after what?"

"The death of the cat. . . . You see my parrot . . ."

"Yes, it's a beautiful bird. . . . Does it talk?"

"It's dead."

"I was surprised that it didn't move for such a long time."

"It was the most intelligent, most affectionate bird in the world. That man was jealous of it. The parrot didn't like him. So, during a fit, I can't call it anything else, a real fit of blind rage, he tore the feathers out of its tail and to mock me put them into a vase."

Madame Martin expressed her disapproval by shaking her head, and at the same time she observed Bouin out of the corner of her eye.

"He looks calm," she muttered, as if to soothe him.

"He appears to be. I'd rather you didn't see him when he is angry. If he hadn't vented his rage on Coco, I'd probably have been his victim."

"Aren't you afraid?"

"You know, at my age . . ."

She must have been rejoicing inwardly, and he suspected her of having rehearsed the scene for a long time. He did not want to leave. It would be like running away.

"Will you come to the kitchen with me? We'll go on chatting while I prepare the tea."

Madame Martin had no desire to remain alone with the man who had just been described to her, and she hastened to follow Marguerite. He could hear the two women talking in low voices, and he wondered what else the old girl would be inventing.

If anything happened to his wife thereafter, the whole neighborhood would consider him guilty. So fine, so gentle, so distinguished a person! A woman who had lived in the same house ever since she was born and whose first husband had been respected by everybody!

Where had she picked up that brute? It's true, isn't it, that one should stick to one's own class?

Actually, where did he come from? Did anyone know? Did anyone know his past?

The women returned. Marguerite was carrying the silver tray that was never used.

"Two lumps of sugar?"

"Please."

"A small cake? These almond cakes. . . . They're excellent."

"Your father was a biscuit manufacturer, wasn't he? It seems to me . . ."

"You're right, Doise Biscuits. That's a whole story in itself. Another story that turned out badly. Almost for the same reasons. He took on, because he was sorry for him, a man who didn't amount to much, someone named Salle-nave. . . . His wife was sick, his son refused to study, he himself was in poor health, in short, the old story. He gave him an important job. Then, when the son was old enough, he took him on too. You may not believe it, but fifteen years later it was my father who found himself at the door of his own business. And half of the alley that they're going to demolish passed into the hands of the Sallenaves. They sold the land. The houses are going to be torn down. An apartment house of I don't know how many stories is going to be put up, and we'll never again see the sun. I'll be lucky if they don't set up a garage and a service station right in front of my windows. As for me, I've re-fused offers. If I had given in, the alley that bears my father's name would disappear. Have another cake."

While Marguerite went on in this feverish vein, Madame Martin kept glancing now at Emile and now at the parrot.

She sensed that there was something abnormal in the atmosphere of the house.

From time to time, she also looked at Marguerite, the way women sometimes look at each other.

Did she perhaps wonder which of the two was not quite right in the head? Perhaps both of them?

VI

He held out for four days, four chaotic days, with the feeling that they were going to win out. It was a conspiracy against his nerves.

Never, in all the years that he had lived in the house, had Marguerite brought in so vulgar a woman as Madame Martin. He now saw her as a veritable neighborhood witch. She had dark eyes, and her lips and cheekbones were reddened by excessive make-up. She wore a dark dress beneath which the structure of a corset could be discerned.

She would arrive at the stroke of four, as she did the first day. He would first hear her steps in the alley. Then she would pass in front of the first window, disappear for a moment and loom up behind the second.

The next moment, the doorbell would ring. He did not

move. He refused to give up any territory to them. He realized that if he yielded an inch, he would gradually lose all his living space.

The invention was diabolical, and he had only to look at Marguerite to be sure that she was pleased with it.

She would go to open the door.

"How nice of you to have come."

"I'm so delighted to chat with you! It's not every day that one meets a woman of your quality. It's so warm today! It's cool in your house. In my apartment, it's stifling, and I have to put up with the neighbors' radio all day long. If only they had taste. But no! All they listen to is silly songs."

"Come in, my dear. Tea's ready."

A glance at Bouin, who was always in his chair in shirt sleeves. He stayed there. He had the right to be there, just as he pleased. It wasn't he who was being visited. They ignored him. Or rather they treated him neither more nor less than like a household animal, like the stuffed parrot in its cage.

"I hope you had a good night?"

"You know, at my age one doesn't need sleep. No sooner do you get into bed than all your troubles rise up."

The witch looked at Emile.

"Have you had new difficulties?"

"It's always the same thing. I've got used to it. If my nerves weren't solid, I'd have been dead or in an asylum long ago."

He hated both of them. For he finally dared admit to himself that he hated his wife. She had brought in outside help. The fight was no longer equal. Who knows if she would not pick up other Madame Martins in the streets and surround herself with a herd of shrews?

He was drinking too much. It was no longer to obtain a moment of pleasant somnolence. He needed a glass or two of wine every hour to give himself courage.

His wife was on the watch. Although he kept the bottles under lock and key in the cupboard, she saw how many he brought back in the morning and she was aware of the reason for his increasingly frequent visits to the kitchen.

Who knows if she did not speak of his drunkenness to anyone who was willing to listen? Madame Martin would serve as a witness. Not having been able to obtain his death and not daring to cause it more directly, perhaps Marguerite was having his funeral in mind?

He was scared. Even when they did not talk about him, he remained in the background of their conversations, which were punctuated with eloquent sighs and looks.

"One can't say, my dear lady, that you've been spoiled by life, and God knows you'd have merited a better one."

"I've never complained. If that's God's will . . ."

"Luckily you have your religion. I always say that when one has religion . . ."

"I pity the people who don't believe in anything."

Her eyes would fix Emile Bouin.

"Don't they lower themselves to the level of animals?"

"That's not quite the same. Animals have no choice."

The tea. The silver tray. The little cakes. Once he went to the kitchen to get a bottle of red wine and a glass and began to drink in front of them.

That was a mistake. He mustn't do it again. His instinct warned him that no good would come of it.

He had got into the habit of going for a drink several times a day at a little bar and grill opposite the prison. The restaurant served meals to well-to-do inmates.

The boss would give such orders as:

"Two pork chops for the Jerk. . . . With a lot of potatoes and salad."

"Chicken in wine sauce for the Notary."

Almost all the prisoners had a nickname. Nobody was surprised that they lived behind bars, between four walls.

"Did they keep My Eye in the infirmary?"

"He got out yesterday. The doctor discovered that he's no more sick than I am."

He would drink his glass of wine at the bar. They did not yet know him, and they were observing him.

"You're not from the neighborhood, are you?"

"I am."

"Your face looks familiar to me."

"I live on Square Sebastian-Doise."

He felt the need to justify his presence, as if he were taking an entrance examination. Unlike at Nelly's place, here there was a continual flow of customers, with some rather strange people among them, who spoke in low voices in the corners, called the boss, whispered in his ear.

"You're not the husband of the old crackpot?"

He nodded, as if the allusion could not be to anyone but Marguerite.

"Why didn't she sell?"

"Sell what?"

"Her houses, of course. There was talk of demolishing the alley to put up a new building. They offered her a fortune, and they had to change all their plans because of her stubbornness."

He returned to Nelly's place too but did not suggest that they go to the kitchen. She realized at once that he was depressed.

"Something wrong?"

"They're doing all they can to get me down. . . . That Madame Martin is a . . . a . . ."

"A rather dark, husky woman with heavy make-up?"

"Yes. . . ."

"The one who was with your wife the other day? Two years ago, she was still telling fortunes. I don't know what happened, but the police went after her. She no longer does anything. It seems that she has money put aside."

"I can't stand them any more."

"Why do you stay with them?"

"Because if I left the room, they'd consider it a victory."

"You're a funny fellow. There are times when I'd swear it amuses you. . . . Are you sure you wouldn't miss your wife?"

"I hate her."

"All right, drink your wine, and try to think about something else, trees, the little birdies."

"I'm serious."

"So am I."

There was even the smell. Madame Martin drenched herself with cheap scent that permeated the living room. Marguerite, who could not bear perfumes, said nothing, which revealed a kind of connivance between them.

He sometimes still followed his wife when she went marketing. She was no longer content with seeing Madame Martin in the afternoon but met her, as if by accident, at the Italian grocery or at the butcher shop, where they stood in line together.

On the morning of the fifth day, he had had enough, and when he entered Nelly's café she realized that he had come not only to drink a glass or two or to spend a moment in the kitchen.

"You look really done in. . . . What have they been up to now?"

"I've got to talk to you."

He was embarrassed and dared not go into detail.

"After all, a man does have his dignity, you realize. . . ."

She laughed to herself. She knew men better than he and knew from experience that when they talk about their dignity it means that things are bad.

"Let me have a drink."

"Is that your fourth glass?"

"You too?"

"Why do you say that?"

"Because my wife keeps count of what I drink. She watches me every moment. It's worse than if I were still a child crawling on all fours. When I come home, she manages to pass near me so that she can smell my breath. The bathroom is the only place where I can lock myself in."

"Poor Emile!"

She took nothing tragically. For her, marital troubles were all alike.

"Well . . . You were talking about your dignity."

"How many rooms do you have upstairs?"

She frowned, for she was not expecting that.

"Two. Why?"

He felt ashamed and continued in a low voice:

"I'm an old fellow, I know. I'm not suggesting that I live with you as . . ."

"As two lovers, I know! In the first place, my boy, I've never been able to sleep with a man. It's a matter of contact, of smell. Making love on the sly, that's all right. But to sweat side by side, to bang against an arm or a leg when I'm not expecting it, no! I tried, in the beginning, with Théo. He was my husband. Because of the business, we got married. Well, after a few days, I asked him to go buy a bed. He slept in the back room. Yet we were fond of each other."

"Did he know you deceived him?"

"What do you mean?"

"Nothing. I beg your pardon. What I'd like is to become a kind of boarder. I'd pay. Name the figure. I wouldn't bother you. I'm not troublesome."

"Would I have to prepare your meals?"

"Perhaps. . . . I'd prefer that. But I'd eat out if I had to."

"For how long?"

"I don't know. Perhaps always."

"Does your old lady bother you as much as that?"

She was thinking.

"How much would you be willing to pay?"

"I don't care. I receive a good pension from the city. I have savings. . . ."

"You won't be hanging around the café all day? The customers don't like that, you realize."

"I know. I'll do whatever you like."

"And what if friends come?"

He looked at the door of the kitchen.

"That's your business."

"You won't get jealous?"

"Why would I get jealous?"

"What you've just said isn't very nice."

"That's true."

"Give me time to think it over."

"How much time?"

"Let's say until you come by tomorrow morning."

"Couldn't it be today?"

"Is it bad as that?"

He did not answer, but he seemed exhausted, and he looked at her entreatingly.

"All right! Come back in half an hour."

"How much do I owe you?"

"Might as well start an account right away."

The same as for the regulars, whose drinks she recorded in a notebook.

"When do you get up?"

"At six o'clock. I can get up at any time. I can take in the garbage cans, open the blinds, sweep the café. I'm used to that."

"Go for a little walk."

He obeyed. He did not remember ever having been so anxious. In his eyes, it was the only possible salvation. At Nelly's place, he would stop thinking about Marguerite and Madame Martin and the threats that hung over him in the house in the alley.

Nelly understood him. She understood everyone. She had no prejudices and saw only the good side of people and events.

The rooms were on the mezzanine and the curved windows could be seen from the sidewalk opposite. The ceiling must be low and probably one could hear all the sounds in the café and the kitchen.

Wasn't it an ideal refuge? He might almost think that he was with Angèle. Nobody would spy on him. He would go out whenever he felt like it without looking back to know whether he was being followed.

The two harpies would no longer be able to run him down in his presence or watch his reactions so as to be able to use them against him.

He walked around the block, first in one direction, then in the other, frequently consulting his watch, and finally he entered the dark, cool café.

There was a customer at the bar, a workman whose smock was spattered with plaster. His face was covered with plaster too, especially his eyebrows and lashes, which made him look like a pierrot.

He was afraid to disturb them. It was not the moment to irritate Nelly. He paused and was about to leave again, but she indicated to him that it was not a customer for the kitchen.

140

"What'll you have?"

"A small white wine, as usual."

"A small one or a big one?"

"A big one."

A trick, in short. He was seventy-one years old and did not have to account to anyone. Why had he said a small one when he knew that she would serve him a big one?

"We still have a week's work in the neighborhood," continued the man. "It's not unpleasant. There are three of us, and we get along well. Can I have a bottle to take to the others?"

"The same?"

She went to draw the wine in the cellar, opened the trap door, and gradually disappeared.

Théo had had a fine life, even if it had ended badly, for he had died young, at the age of sixty-two or three.

"Thanks."

The plasterer could not help letting his eyes rest on the rounded bosom. If he worked another week in the area, he would probably take advantage of her like the others. He was fair-haired, not more than thirty, and had laughing eyes.

"Well?"

"Let's give it a try."

"When can I come?"

"Whenever you like. I just have to remake the bed. No one has slept in it since Théo died."

He did not ask about the price.

"I'll bring my suitcase right away, after lunch."

"You're not going to move all your things, I hope."

He was so relieved that he felt like whistling in the street. It was a deliverance, and he wondered how he had not thought of Nelly earlier.

When he entered the house, his eyes were sparkling with mischief. Marguerite was going to have the surprise of her life. Her victim was escaping her. She would find herself alone, without anyone to spy on, and he tried to imagine the conversation that the two women would have that afternoon when they drank their tea.

"Did he take everything?" that snake of a Madame Martin would ask.

"No. Only a big suitcase."

"Perhaps he went on a trip? Someone sick or dead out of town? . . ."

"He has no family left. He never gets letters, only advertisements."

"How did he look?"

"As if he were mocking me."

"I'm sure he'll be back."

"Do you think so?"

"Didn't you follow him?"

She must have blushed, for she had actually followed him. But he had played a good trick on her, thus proving that he had regained his equilibrium.

The suitcase was heavy. He had lugged it to Place Saint-Jacques, where there were always two or three taxis.

Marguerite did not hide herself. She walked about ten yards behind him; when he turned around, he could see the distraught look on her face.

"You'll see, old girl."

In her haste, she had neglected to take her handbag. She was therefore without money. He had stepped into the first taxi, and had called out to the driver:

"East Station."

The station from which he had left for the front in 1914.

She stood there at the edge of the sidewalk not trusting her eyes. After a few minutes, he leaned forward and said, "Drive around for a little while, anywhere. Then I'll tell you where to go."

"What about the East Station?"

"I've changed my mind."

"You're the one who's paying."

Finally he murmured, calculating that Marguerite had had time to return home:

"At the corner of Rue des Feuillantines."

"What corner?"

"Whichever you please."

A hot sun was shining. Paris smelled good. It was years since he had smelled the odors of the city as he was smelling them now.

He had played a good practical joke. She would at last realize that he was not a household pet that one buys and domesticates.

She was in the process of eating, alone at the table, alone in the kitchen, alone in the house, posing as someone who isn't hungry, who never has an appetite.

A pure spirit floating above vulgar contingencies!

"Already? You said . . ."

Nelly was eating, alone too, but with a hearty appetite.

"I'll drop off my suitcase and leave. I didn't have the patience to wait and have lunch again in her presence. I'll go to the restaurant."

She hesitated to propose that he share her meal, which was appetizing, Toulouse sausages cooked in red cabbage. They were plump and juicy and smelled agreeably of garlic.

She preferred not to create a precedent. She was a practical woman, with both feet planted firmly on the ground. She knew men. If she got along with them, it was because she did not ask them for more than they could give.

"Have a pleasant meal."

"You too."

He smiled at her gratefully and went off feeling rejuvenated.

Throughout his life, often without realizing it, he had made for himself a series of habits, a more or less rigorous schedule.

It would last for weeks, months, or years and would then give way, for no apparent reason, to a different rhythm, other rules, other schedules.

There had been the life in his parents' home, first as a young man, then in the early days of his marriage with Angèle. It had not always been easy, for his mother found her daughter-in-law's presence a burden. As for his father, he was prudent or resigned and avoided interfering.

His mother, in particular, was strict about mealtimes, and when she was cooking she did not want anyone under her feet.

144

"Go for a walk. I don't want you getting in my way."

Consequently, they spent a great deal of time out of doors. They would walk. They knew the quays from Charenton to the Pont Neuf, and they would sometimes stroll along them late at night.

When they rented their apartment, above a café, they often ate in the restaurant, either because Angèle had got up too late or because they wanted a special dish. They enjoyed discovering pleasant, inexpensive little places where the customers' napkins were kept in individual pigeonholes.

There had been a time when they frequented the Mélanie, near the Wine Market; then the Père Charles, Rue Saint-Louis-en-l'Ile, and others. Each had its very own smell and colors.

It had been the same on Sundays. One spring he bought a motorcycle on which they drove to the Forest of Fontainebleau, but after barely avoiding an accident, Angèle had been frightened and he sold the machine.

For two years they had regularly taken the train to Lagny, and they knew all the pleasant places in the area. They had danced in the country cabarets. He had taken up fishing, and his wife had tried to emulate him.

Then there had been the hospital, where he would arrive ahead of visiting hours. He would sit on the same bench and read the evening paper which he had just bought, grumbling when the bell announced the time for visits before he had read the headlines.

His solitary life in the alley as a widower, the novels he had devoured near the window, the screams of the baby downstairs, the games of cards in the afternoons at the Denfert-Rochereau café . . .

Marguerite . . .

And now he was once again in a new world into which he was trying to integrate himself.

Nelly's room looked out on the street, but his did not. From his window he could see only another window, which was so dirty that it was not possible to guess what there was behind it.

Somewhere, in an invisible workshop, a hammer kept striking metal in a slow, regular rhythm.

He did not complain. He was happy to have escaped the atmosphere of the alley.

"What do you do with your days?"

"I walk, I read. . . ."

"If you don't see well enough in your room, you can sit in mine, near the window, providing you don't smoke your awful cigars."

He did not resent her saying that, as he had resented Marguerite's attitude.

"I'd like to lend you a hand."

"We'll see about it."

He could guess from the look on her face that she was not too pleased about having accepted his presence.

"You're an odd fellow."

He had bought secondhand books, five or six, quite a stock. For the first time, he had returned to the café on Place Denfert-Rochereau. The boss had recognized him.

"Welcome back! Have you been sick?"

He looked at him with solicitude, as if Bouin were not

looking well. It was true that he had lost a great deal of weight.

It was particularly obvious at the neck. His shirt collars yawned and revealed a prominent Adam's apple with skin sagging on both sides.

He looked toward the table near the window where his friends had been in the habit of playing cards.

"Are you looking for the old-timers? Big Désiré died a year ago. The Colonel, as they called him, though he had only been a sergeant . . ."

"What was the matter with him?"

"It happened in the street. . . . The stout little fellow . . . Wait. His name is on the tip of my tongue. . . . Loireau? . . . Voiron? . . . The one who had the stationery store at Porte d'Orléans . . . It doesn't matter. . . . He went back to his village in Dordogne. . . . I don't know what's become of the others. They come and go. . . . What'll you have?"

"A red Bordeaux."

"Joseph! A red Bordeaux. And you? Everything all right with you?"

"I'm not complaining."

"Your wife died, didn't she? As the result of an accident? . . . You see, I remember my customers. Sometimes the name escapes me, but I remember the faces. Do you still live in the neighborhood?"

"Near Place Saint-Jacques."

"It's not you who . . . I remember! . . . You married the owner of a whole alley."

"Only of a row of houses," he corrected.

"All the same, that's quite a pile. They're building a new apartment house opposite, isn't that right?"

"Not yet. The work hasn't begun. Certain tenants aren't moving out until next month."

"Would you like some partners for a game?"

"Not particularly."

He did not know the players who had taken the place of those of the old days. They were younger.

"They're bridge players. They stay until eight o'clock. . . . The belote players arrive around four."

He returned to Rue des Feuillantines by a long detour in order to go through Montsouris Park. He almost went by Rue de la Santé to catch a glimpse of the house at the end of the alley, but it was a ridiculous idea and he gave it up.

He entered by the tenants' hallway, opened the door of the kitchen a crack, and called out, "I'm going up."

He was being discreet. He had hardly arrived and was afraid that Nelly might tire of his presence. It was better to live on tiptoe. He read, went out for a moment to smoke a cigar, went back, and watched people go by in the street.

He liked the smell in Nelly's room, a rather strong smell, that reminded him of the brief moments with her in the kitchen.

At about seven, he went down again to have dinner. She was behind the bar, facing a half-dozen customers. He read his newspaper while he was eating, imagined Marguerite all alone in her kitchen, unless she had invited Madame Martin.

It would have amused him to hide in a corner when

Madame Martin arrived in the afternoon at the stroke of four.

Marguerite must have sighed: "Good riddance!"

"It's a shame after all you've done for him. When I think that you picked him up the way one picks up a cat in the street . . ."

If Madame Martin had said that, she had made a blunder, for it was preferable not to mention cats in the house. Perhaps she had spoken of a dog.

"Aren't you a little afraid, in his state of mind . . ."

"Afraid of what?"

"I don't know. . . . A man who's not all there . . ."

Had his wife heard when he had told the driver to take him to the East Station? If so, she would wonder where he might be going. He knew nobody east of Paris, neither in the suburbs nor in the more distant cities. It was only because of the First World War that he had taken a train at that station. Later, with Angèle, he had never gone any farther than Lagny. When he got back, Nelly was eating at one end of the table.

"Did you have a good dinner?"

"A steak and fried potatoes."

"I love fried potatoes, but I never make them because they smell up the place and the customers don't like that. I sometimes go out and eat them on Sunday, when I make up my mind to leave the house."

"What do you do the other times?"

"I sleep, I listen to the radio, I read, not much, because I don't care much for books. The stories are always the same, and there's almost nothing true about them."

"When do you close?"

"When I feel like going to bed. Hardly anyone comes in the evening. A customer from time to time. For a quick drink."

"I'll be going."

"Why?"

"I'm afraid of disturbing you. . . . I promised you I wouldn't."

"Actually you're shy. I'd never have thought it. You didn't go prowling around Rue de la Santé by any chance?"

"What on earth for?"

"I don't know. Maybe to get a glimpse of your wife, to see how she took the shock. You want me to tell you something? You both need each other as much as two newly-weds. Don't say no. You'll see. You'll be back with her in two weeks."

"I'd rather . . . I don't know what . . . Anything . . ."

"All right, then I'm wrong. You know what? While I do my dishes, you can put out the garbage cans. You'll find them in the yard, at the end of the hallway. The ones with a red circle. Each tenant has his color or initials, otherwise we'd get mixed up and drag around some other person's garbage."

She read the newspaper. She was interrupted twice by customers, and both times he left in the event that she needed the kitchen.

"Say, stop going in and out like the weather man in a Swiss barometer. What do you think? That I offer my ass as a tribute to all my customers? All right! You're not the only one, and there'll be others. But since I do it to please myself, I have the right to choose."

They went upstairs at about ten o'clock. It was he who had closed the blinds.

"Do you go to bed early too?"

"Yes, unless there's an interesting program on television."

"I don't have television. It's expensive."

He promised himself that he would buy her a set the next day. It would be pleasant to watch the programs in the evening at her side.

Without realizing it, he was already building up a little world rather similar to the one which he had just fled.

"I don't have a bathtub, only a shower. That door over there. The water's not heated in summer. It's true that you don't need hot water. . . ."

She was taking off her dress. The door between the rooms was open. He removed his jacket and took off his tie and waited hesitantly before undressing further.

"What did you do this afternoon?"

"I had a drink at Denfert-Rochereau. A café where I used to play cards almost every day. The old-timers have scattered. . . . I don't know the newcomers."

"And then?"

"I went to Montsouris Park and sat on a bench."

"Watching the children play?"

She was poking fun at him.

"Or throwing crumbs to the little birds?"

"Why do you laugh at me?"

"For no reason. . . . Life's funny. . . . Don't you

think it's funny? Look, here you are, good as gold, so I don't shut the door before I'm all undressed. You know my ass, but you've never seen me naked. Confess!"

"Yes. . . . I often thought about it at night."

"While trying to fall asleep in your own wife's room! All right, if you feel like it, we'll inaugurate your stay by making love. Not on my bed or in my room. . . . In yours. . . ."

When she was naked, she put away her clothes, moving about without embarrassment.

"Well?"

"All right . . . ," he murmured.

"Are you staying like that?"

He was still wearing his shirt and trousers.

"I'd rather . . ."

He did not dare undress any further. His face might possibly give a different impression, but his skinny body was that of an old man, and he was afraid of a pitying or mocking look.

"Do you want me to lie down or what?"

In spite of the presence of the bed, they ended by doing just as they did behind the door.

"All right! Now I'm going to shut myself in and sleep. Good night."

She mockingly kissed him on the forehead, and retired to her room where he heard her get into bed.

The following day was much the same, with the difference that in the evening the television set was already installed in the kitchen. When the set was delivered, Nelly's way of thanking him was to say:

"You're not so dumb."

"Why?"

"Oh, no reason. . . . That'll give us something to do in the evening. Did you and your old lady watch television?"

"Yes."

"And with the other one?"

"We didn't have it yet."

On Sunday morning, she stayed in bed until eleven o'clock, and when she opened the door she was still half asleep.

"Haven't you gone out?"

"I was waiting for you to get up. I want to invite you to lunch in a good restaurant, wherever you like, in Paris or out in the country."

"Are you as rich as that?"

"It would give me pleasure. You'll be able to eat fried potatoes."

"How about Saint-Cloud? There used to be a kind of place where you could dance, with real arbors. I went there with Théo. I wonder whether it's still there."

They took the subway. It was the first time he had ever seen her out of doors. She was wearing a cotton dress and white shoes. They looked for the dance hall along the Seine and finally found it, and they had to wait almost an hour in order to get a table.

"Do you know how old I was the first time I came here?"

"Twenty?"

"Eighteen . . . I was still a whore on Boulevard Sébastopol. Théo picked me up as he would have picked up any other girl. There were three of us girls at the same street corner, and in the darkness he chose at random. . . . When it was over, he didn't leave right away. He started asking me questions. I didn't like that. . . . There are loads of guys who pay a girl just so she'll tell them her life story, and others who weep over their own troubles. . . . He came back, invited me to lunch, and brought me here, I'll have you know, in a taxi! . . . I had no idea that I'd be married to him three months later. Isn't that a riot? And now here I am in the same place with you, who . . ."

She did not continue. He would have liked to know what she had been about to say, but he dared not insist.

When they got back, after walking along the Seine and looking at the barges, she said, "All right, you can eat with me here this time. . . . On Sunday evening I make do with ham and cheese."

They watched television. She did not understand the serial because she had not seen the earlier shows, and he told her what it was about. They did not go upstairs until eleven o'clock and separated immediately.

"I'm in a hurry to get into bed. I bet I'm sunburned. I so rarely go out."

He had surprised her on Monday morning by sweeping the tiles, tidying up the kitchen, and preparing coffee before she came down. He was behaving somewhat like a dog that has found a new master and tries to please him. He, too, was afraid of being kicked out into the street, and he suspected that Nelly's infatuations did not always last long.

She put up with him, found the situation amusing. How long would it last? He made himself inconspicuous, rendered little services, and hastened to disappear when he was no longer needed.

He returned to Montsouris Park, where he did watch the children play. He had not had children himself. As for his friends, or rather his cronies, he would meet them in the café, rarely at home, or else it was in the evening and the children were in bed.

He observed them with amazement, as if he were discovering youth after the age of seventy. What surprised him most was the tough speech they used in front of their indifferent mothers.

Had it been like this when he was young? At the age of thirteen, he would not have dared tell his mother that he had learned from fellow pupils how babies were born.

Sit up straight. . . . Don't put your finger into your nose. . . . Eat properly. . . . Where did you pick up all that mud? . . . Wipe your feet. . . .

If he had had children, they would be married by now, would have children of their own.

Would Bouin be happier if he had had them? Was he unhappy? Had he ever been really unhappy in his life?

Square Sebastian-Doise? Obviously. There had been that period. He had fretted and fumed, especially since the matter of the cat. His wife hated him. He hated her too. One day when she had constantly been putting her hand to her chest as if her heart were going to stop beating, he had written a note to her:

YOU CAN CROAK.

Did he really mean it? In any case, it was a reaction to her nastiness. She found subtler things to say to him and diabolically managed to put him in the wrong.

It was established once and for all that he was a monster and she an innocent victim.

What was the use of thinking about it now? He had escaped from her. He was free. He liked the little café with the red tiles, the kitchen that smelled good, the two rooms, the place that was already his during the day, near the curved window.

It was pleasant to see Nelly open her door in the morning, heavy with sleep, in her creased nightgown and, in the evening, leave the door open while she undressed.

"Will you sell me a bottle of red Bordeaux? I sometimes feel like having a drink upstairs and I don't want to disturb you."

"Corked wine at a franc a glass?"

"Right."

"I'll get it from the cellar a little later."

There! Life was getting organized. He had found a new spot for himself.

VII

It lasted a little more than a week, exactly ten days, including two Sundays, the one when they went to Saint-Cloud and the Sunday of the storm which they had spent dawdling on the ground floor and upstairs, finally ending up, bored and sullen, in front of the television set.

Later, he probably would have difficulty admitting that his life with Nelly had been so short, for, in his mind, Nelly was to join the women with whom he had lived for a long time, his mother, Angèle, Marguerite.

She would end up by merging with the others.

It was hard to explain. He remembered words, gestures, phrases, particularly looks, and even more his reaction to those looks, but he did not know whether it was an unconscious memory of one or the other of the lives that he had led.

One morning, around ten o'clock, he was reading the paper near the sickle-shaped window.

He read more papers than in the past because he lacked the courage to start a long novel. One had to read a certain number of pages to familiarize oneself with the characters and their names, and he was often obliged to turn back.

There were more slack hours than in the alley, for he made a point of not disturbing Nelly when customers might drop in. He went for long walks. That was not enough to fill his days. He continued sitting on a bench in Montsouris Park, and he had lunch and dinner out except on the two occasions when he had been asked to stay.

That morning, he raised his eyes and saw her on the opposite sidewalk. It was Marguerite. She was standing there motionless, with her shopping bag in her hand, and looked at him with a pained expression that was new to him.

He was so struck that he almost spoke, as if there were no distance between them. The window was open. If he had raised his voice, she would have heard him.

He had not imagined her like that. Her stiffness and assurance had disappeared. She was no longer the former Mademoiselle Doise, but a worn-out, tired, anxious, and perhaps sick woman.

She had hastily put on an old dress that did not become her. And she had aged.

Was he mistaken, or were Marguerite's lips actually moving as if in prayer?

He was disturbed and embarrassed and tried not to stand up, not to move. He tried to look away. People passed on the narrow sidewalk and grazed and pushed her as they went by. She watched, fascinated, and did not move.

Then, slowly and regretfully, she trudged to the corner of Rue Saint-Antoine.

He had remained in his chair a good quarter of an hour without reading his paper. He had gone down. Nelly was at the bar serving the locksmith from the end of the street.

"A glass of white wine."

She observed him with curiosity, served him with a mechanical gesture, and continued what she was saying:

". . . if there's been one, there'll be others. . . . The weather is murky, and it'll be a few days before it clears up. . . ."

He finally gathered that she was talking about the storms. There had been one the night before, the third in four days.

"All I want," grumbled the locksmith, "is nice weather on Sunday. I promised the kids to take them to the country, and . . ."

He went off wiping his mouth. Nelly and Bouin looked at each other.

"Well?" she asked.

"Well what?"

"Don't tell me you haven't seen her?"

"I did."

"What did it do to you?"

"Nothing. . . . Why?"

She too pretended that she could read his thoughts. He resented it. It annoyed him to discover that she was like the others.

He had not come downstairs in order to confess. He did

not know why he had come down. Certainly not to hide behind his mother's skirts.

He almost murmured:

"She's aged a lot."

He said nothing, for she would deduce that he felt pity. For the first time, he was not at ease in Nelly's presence, and he began to have doubts about her.

"Where are you going?"

"For a walk."

Not to join Marguerite. He went in the opposite direction. He tried not to think about her.

It was an unpleasant day. He spent more time at the window than on the other days. All the same, he went to Montsouris Park, where he remained on his bench only a few minutes.

He was expecting it. The next day, at the same time, he saw her in the same place, in almost exactly the same pose. Her eyes were raised, and there was something pathetic about that frail little old woman who made him think of those one sees in churches addressing their prayers to the statue of the Virgin.

This time, Nelly did not refer to her, but she was not as much at ease with him as she had been. She seemed to be thinking:

"My boy, you're in a bad way."

It was true. He was upset. He had thought that he had freed himself, and he was beginning to discover that it was only an illusion.

She returned a third time, a fourth. She looked heart-rendingly frail, as if she were about to drop to the sidewalk with exhaustion. One afternoon, in the street, he turned around mechanically and saw that she was following a hundred feet behind him.

It was the hour for Montsouris Park. He did not change either his habits or his itinerary. He stepped out briskly as always. He heard hurried little footsteps behind him, and after a while he slowed down because she must have been winded.

She was visibly suffering. She missed him. She had lost her equilibrium in the empty house, and her presence behind him was an admission, a prayer.

He tried hard not to be moved. He sat down on his bench while she remained standing at the corner of a walk.

"Did you go there?"

Nelly questioned him when he got back. How could she have guessed that Marguerite had followed him, that he had been tempted to . . .

"No."

"You know, Emile, you mustn't worry about me. . . . I'll understand. . . ."

He resented her saying that. He had always hated being judged, and it annoyed him even more when people foresaw what he was going to do while he himself did not know and was debating inwardly.

He did not want to return to the alley. He was happy here. He had his little ways and habits.

But he no longer had the feeling of release he had had the first few days.

He had almost succeeded in forgetting about Marguerite.

And now she was imposing herself upon him, timidly, with a humility he would never have suspected of her.

Had Madame Martin advised her to act this way? Did the two women still see each other every afternoon in order to talk about him?

He asked himself questions, these and many others, to the detriment of his peace of mind.

"Are you going out?"

"I need air. It's been a stifling day."

That evening, at nightfall, he headed almost directly, with a detour that was just sufficient to make him seem to hesitate, for Rue de la Santé, and he passed in front of the alley, saw the lamppost, and heard the jet of water. He was unable to tell from a distance whether or not there was a light in one of the windows of the last house.

Nelly did not ask him anything. When he got back, she was in bed. He shut the door of his room, mumbling in a very low voice, in case she had fallen asleep:

"Good night."

"Good night."

It was a bad night. He got up at least five times, gave himself the excuse of having to urinate, and fell asleep again each time with difficulty. He got involved in labyrinthine dreams which he was unable to remember when he awoke. All he knew was that he thrashed about. He was resisting something. He was unable to tell what it was that he was resisting so fiercely, but he was overwhelmed at the fact that everyone was against him and that he stood alone.

At six o'clock he got up, worn out, swept away the sawdust, washed the kitchen floor, and took in the garbage cans. He drank red wine from a bottle, and when Nelly came down in house slippers and practically naked under her black dress, he found nothing to say to her.

She came, as he expected, she stood exactly in the same spot, in the same pose, and turned the same questioning look upon him, the memory of which he was unable to shake off.

Her eyes were pale blue, but when she was upset the blue turned a dirty gray, and her face lost all its luminosity and became a sickly ivory.

She looked as if she were extinguished, as if she were no longer struggling.

He refused again to let himself be influenced, but he was not quite successful. He was not hungry at lunchtime and left half of his meal on his plate, though he had chosen his favorite restaurant and ordered a veal dish of which he was particularly fond.

"Anything wrong with it?" asked the proprietor anxiously.

"No, but I'm not hungry."

"It's the heat. You don't seem to be able to take the heat."

He, too, scrutinized him as if to detect on his face the traces of God knows what ailment.

Couldn't they leave him alone? He did not have to justify himself to anyone, and everyone was observing and judging him.

Was he judging Nelly? Had he ever judged Angèle, his mother, Marguerite?

He finally got angry, lumped them all together, regarding them as enemies. Now, if men did the same . . .

He did not return home but jumped on a passing bus. He got off on Boulevard Saint-Michel and made for the quays. He walked for a long time, but without looking at the barges that were unloading, a thing that had always fascinated him.

He hardly looked at his former house. As for the home of his parents, of his childhood, behind the lock at Charenton, it had long since been demolished to make way for a low-cost housing project.

He was too tired to walk to Rue des Feuillantines. He waited for a bus, feeling sullen and anxious. He had a smell of dust in his nostrils, and his shoes hurt him. He had not taken such a long walk in years.

He almost entered by the hallway, but he finally went into the café. Nelly was not behind the bar. He noticed a moving shadow behind the curtain of the kitchen door.

He felt no jealousy. She joined him, straightening out the bottom of her dress; a few minutes later, a man appeared on the sidewalk, his face ostensibly turned the other way.

"She came. . . ."

He said nothing. He had nothing to say.

"She seemed confused. . . ."

Perhaps because he had not taken his usual walk to Montsouris Park. Perhaps she thought he was sick.

"This time, she crossed the street."

"Did she come in?"

"No. . . . She almost did. . . . She touched the lamp-post with her fingers. . . . She looked at me as if she were going to photograph me, then she turned away and left."

He did not ask:

"How did she look?"

He realized what an effort it had been for Marguerite to cross the street and approach the house. She had been on the point of entering. . . . She would have been obliged to talk to Nelly. What would she have said? . . . Would she have dared ask for news about him? . . . Would she have begged Nelly to give him back to her?

"You'd better make up your mind."

"About what?"

She shrugged, as if he were a child asking a foolish question.

"The two of you are playing cat-and-mouse."

"I don't know what you mean."

"You know very well, and you know how it will end."

"How?"

She shrugged again.

"Here! Drink. . . ."

They hardly said a word to each other as they watched television. It was as if each were alone in front of the screen. They went upstairs and said good night on the landing.

He slept better, though still oppressed, but he was less agitated than the night before. It was Nelly whom he now resented. He did the morning chores mechanically, and when she came down they avoided looking at each other.

Marguerite was there again at ten o'clock. He did not look her in the face either. His gaze became shifty, as if he wanted to keep a secret that the others were trying to wrest from him.

She finally left. His eyes followed her until she disappeared at the corner.

There were customers downstairs. He could hear the cheerful voices of the workmen who were treating each other to drinks during the morning break. He had done the same kind of thing when he was in charge of jobs and would accompany a foreman or contractor to a bar.

He was standing in front of Nelly's bed, a brass bed of the kind that was common when he was young. He went back to his room and opened his wardrobe, where he kept a bottle of red Bordeaux which he himself had drawn from the barrel in the cellar.

Like Théo . . . Théo who was dead . . . Death had taken him suddenly, when he was not expecting it, as it had taken his mother.

It would happen to him. . . . It could happen at any moment to Marguerite, who had returned to her house and was alone in the kitchen.

Who would discover her body? And when?

He struggled and tried not to give in. Nelly was right. He really knew how it all would end. Then why not end it all now?

She was laughing downstairs at a coarse joke of one of the customers, but he was sure that she was listening to his footsteps on the floor above.

The suitcase was on top of the wardrobe. He reached up to get it, took his clothes off the hangers, and jumbled his linen with his extra pair of shoes.

He didn't care about what she would say or the way she would look at him. He was tired of being the object of other people's comments. He had the right to live as he saw fit, to follow his impulses.

He looked at himself in the mirror and thought he looked old.

What was the use of understanding? He had questioned himself during the last few days until his head ached.

He went down the stairs slowly, with his suitcase in his hand. He could have gone off without being seen, could have gone directly to the street and turned left.

He owed her money. He had not paid for his room or for the bottles he had emptied or for the glasses he had drunk at the bar.

The workmen had gone. The only one left was the plasterer with the head of a clown. He had become a regular visitor. Had he been on the other side of the door, with his eye on the kitchen curtain?

Nelly looked at him without manifesting any surprise.

"I suppose you want your bill?"

She was not angry. She spoke to him as usual. She looked for his page in the notebook.

"I'm not going to count the room."

"I insist."

"I don't know what it's worth nor even how many days you stayed."

"Eleven."

She seemed surprised that he had counted.

"Have it your own way. Let's say three francs a day."

"That's too little. At least five."

"Let's not argue about it. Fifty-two francs for your drinks."

"Plus two meals."

"Then I ought to deduct the lunch at Saint-Cloud. . . . You were my guest."

The red-headed plasterer waited without quite understanding what was going on. Bouin took a bill from his wallet.

"Have you got the change?"

"Not enough."

There was none in the cashbox either.

"I'll go get some."

She left, crossed a spot of sunlight, and went to the pastry shop, the bell of which tinkled as she entered.

"Here we are! I think that does it. A Sancerre?"

He could not refuse. She poured herself a glass too.

"This one's on the house," she said ironically.

He gulped down his drink and muttered a clumsy farewell. He left without turning around, feeling the eyes of Nelly and her companion on his back.

In a moment, they would be making love behind the door, and the thought pinched his heart.

He followed the familiar itinerary, one that he had followed for years. In the yard of the hospital, women, children, and old people were standing in line in front of the door of the dispensary. Farther off, a Black Maria was waiting in front of the prison.

He turned to the left, into the alley. On one side, the houses were empty. The blinds were closed on the ground floor. The windows on the upper floor were without curtains.

The line that separated light and shadow ran right down the middle of the gutter.

He did not use the key, which he had kept without meaning to. He put down his suitcase on the sidewalk and rang the bell. He listened attentively and was surprised by the silence inside. He started when the door opened and when he saw half of a face through a slight opening.

He had prepared a slip of paper which he did not flick with the familiar movement of the thumb and middle finger. When the door opened wide, he handed it to her without a word.

Marguerite took it. She did not say anything, but looked anxious. She took her glasses from the pocket of her apron. She read it and, leaving the door open, entered the living room.

He crossed the threshold and recognized the smell and density of the air. In the living room, he saw the cage and the rigid parrot.

Marguerite was leaning over the piano and writing. His note was a question:

MADAME MARTIN?

And also a condition for his surrender. He was not coming back with his ears stinging. He was not begging for permission to resume his place in the house.

He was tempted to go upstairs at once and empty his suitcase, but he prepared to wait. Marguerite did not hand him the message which she had just written. She placed it on the piano. Sitting in her armchair, she picked up her knitting as if to make him realize that nothing had changed.

He walked over hesitantly and put out his hand:

I KICKED THE HARPY OUT.

She waited a long moment before raising her eyes to see whether he was satisfied. Then, as if nothing had happened during the last two weeks, she began knitting again and moving her lips.

It was not until the following spring that the demolition began. To begin with, cars drew up in front of the empty houses for several days, and groups of strangers kept coming and going. At times, workmen were with them, and occasionally one was startled to see them appear on the roofs, engaged in some kind of mysterious work.

Marguerite was very nervous and kept going to the window to watch every half-hour.

One morning when they went to do their marketing, one following the other, they found a cordon of police on Rue de la Santé. Bouin thought at first that a prisoner had escaped, but when he returned, still following his wife at a distance of ten yards, he understood.

An attempt was being made to get a huge crane into the alley, and a crowd had gathered to witness the spectacle. The tractor moved forward, stopped, backed up, and started again cautiously, while a whole crew busied itself all about.

Marguerite went by disdainfully. He found her purchases abandoned on the kitchen table. When he went upstairs, he discovered that she had locked herself in the bedroom and he heard her crying.

It took the entire day to bring the crane as far as the front of their house, and the bronze Eros was almost knocked over.

A painful period was beginning. The following day, a truck brought a huge iron ball to the site.

For two months, it was like a circus. The first blow was given on a Monday. The preceding days, veritable acrobats balanced themselves on the roofs and then on the beams and fragments of walls and tossed armfuls of tiles into the alley, where they broke in a great din.

He felt like saying:

"Don't stay at the window."

Every new noise made her start, and she put her hand to her chest twenty times a day, as if she were suffering from a heart disease.

When the ball rose into the air, they both watched, each at a bedroom window. Down below, a man in a leather jacket had a whistle in his mouth. The alley was blocked off by a red and white barrier.

The ball first swung in the void like a pendulum, describing an arc that kept getting larger. At its highest point, it almost reached the walls. The progression was slow. Finally it struck, and a crack ran down house number 8 from top to bottom.

He was almost sure that he would hear Marguerite's scream, but he could not be sure because of the din.

The ball returned, struck again, and a wall collapsed in a cloud of dust. A fireplace remained suspended in space, stuck to what was left of a room with yellow-striped wallpaper.

The rubble had to be carried off day after day. The trucks worked in relays. When Marguerite and Bouin returned from their marketing, they were obliged to tell who they were, for only the residents of the alley were allowed to pass.

At five o'clock, everything fortunately calmed down, but it all began again the following morning at seven o'clock. Floors hung in mid-air for two or three days. A flight of stairs led nowhere.

And men were always doing acrobatic tricks as they stood out against the sky.

The houses were knocked down one after the other and left holes like decayed teeth. Marguerite shuddered as she looked at them.

Several times during that period, he almost spoke to her; he wanted to say something, anything, appeasing words. He realized that it was too late now and that neither of them could turn back.

She even became aggressive again after sleepless nights. One day, eager to watch the demolition, in which he had come to take a passionate interest, he did not take his shower. Later in the day, he found a note on the piano.

YOU'D BETTER TAKE A SHOWER.
YOU SMELL BAD.

Neither of them had the right to disarm. The game had become their life. It was as natural and necessary for them to send venomous notes to each other as for others to exchange pleasant words or kisses.

He was sure that he hated her, even if he did sometimes pity her. However, he did not hold it against her that she had brought him back to the alley by trickery, by displaying false anguish beneath the window on Rue des Feuillantines.

Several times since then, he had seen a quickly repressed smile on her lips, no doubt when she thought about her victory.

She had triumphed over a woman much younger than she, a woman with whom he certainly made love.

She, the old woman, as the two of them must have called her, had therefore lost none of her power.

The crane departed, with the same difficulties as when it had arrived. It left behind heaps of broken bricks, plaster, scrap metal, and rubbish of all kinds, and then, for a month, there was no one on the premises. There was silence, complete calm, except at night when the rats began to prowl around the garbage cans.

To be sure, there was almost nobody in the row of untouched houses. Everybody was in the country or at the seashore, some in Spain or Italy.

Even for someone other than Marguerite, someone who had not been born in the alley and lived all his life there, it was a depressing sight, to say nothing of the smell, a pervasive indefinable smell that recalled that of cemeteries where new graves have just been dug.

At the beginning of September, the trucks came back and the crane started functioning again to remove the rubble. When it was over, all that remained was the spectacle of the cellars, where a few sets of shelves and a broken barrel still lingered.

The crews changed, as did the gestures and accents of the workmen.

It was now the turn of the excavators and the power drills, and Bouin, deafened by the noise, resumed the habit of spending part of the afternoon in Montsouris Park. He would take a book and sit on a bench, his former bench in the time of Nelly.

After two days, Marguerite, who must have followed him, sat down on another bench, almost opposite him, with her eternal knitting.

Tenants rang at the door, and he could hear them complaining vehemently in the living room.

There was nothing she could do about it. She was not even able to tell them when the work would be over, and the family from number 5 moved two weeks later. The house remained empty, despite an advertisement in the newspaper.

The contractors must have fallen behind schedule. Instead of finishing at five o'clock, the work continued until seven, and when the days grew shorter they installed electric floodlights.

Was it a matter of bad organization? Suddenly the site was a veritable anthill in upheaval and then, abruptly, there was no one on the job for weeks. In the café where Bouin went for his glass of wine, people said that the construction company had run out of funds and that the work would be taken over by another firm with the help of a big bank.

Whom was one to believe? There were all sorts of rumors. The winter went by with alternating periods of deafening noise and silence.

Marguerite dragged about like someone who has received a fatal blow. She was more and more colorless, and when she did her marketing, she sometimes stopped to put her hand on her chest and forced a smile so that the passersby would not notice.

She did not want people to pity her or ask her questions about her health. When she stopped in the street, she pretended to be looking at a window. Then she would walk on with a less assured gait.

Perhaps she was simply putting on an act for Emile. He knew she was capable of it, and that was why he was never alarmed for very long.

When the butcher's wife asked her, "Aren't you well, Madame Bouin? You look a bit tired," she had replied, "I'm fine. Let me have a very small cutlet."

The butcher's wife was from the South, and in her language, being a bit tired meant being at death's door.

Bouin also began to feel the effects of what was going on and started walking almost as she did. He would start and sigh as soon as one of the machines began to operate.

He avoided Rue des Feuillantines, made an effort not to think about it. What was stranger was the fact that that thin slice of his life now seemed to him almost incredible.

He had difficulty convincing himself that he had really lived there, that he had been free, that he had played at being the keeper of a café, and that at night an opulent woman with firm flesh undressed in front of him without any shame.

He had only to say a word, to make a gesture . . .

They had had lunch together one Sunday at Saint-Cloud, in a dance hall, like lovers, like a young couple. . . .

Then, to take revenge, he took out his notebook with the thin slips of paper and printed in block letters:

THE CAT.

VIII

How much time had gone by since the morning, when, in spite of the flu, he had gone down to the cellar and found the stiff corpse of his cat?

He did not know exactly. The dates got mixed up. Besides, it was of no importance. Three years? Two years?

There had been Madame Martin. He had seen her again only once, from a distance, several months before. But she had probably left the neighborhood, or else she did her marketing elsewhere.

There had been Nelly. . . .

There had been Marguerite on the sidewalk opposite. . . .

There had been the ball that swung against the sky and

struck the walls between which human beings had lived and which still bore their traces. . . .

There had been wind, rain, hail, snow. . . .

The excavator had dug deeply into the ground. It had encountered pipes and cables and had burst a sewer pipe which had smelled up the neighborhood for three days.

There had been workmen with various accents, Italians, Spaniards, and, in the end, Turks. . . .

There had been fierce notes from both Marguerite and himself. . . .

There had been . . .

He was alive. He would get up at six o'clock, take his shower, shave, go downstairs, bring in the garbage can, then do his part of the household chores after drinking one and more often two or three glasses of wine.

Then the wood. He mustn't forget to split wood. He mustn't forget anything. The routine had to be followed scrupulously.

November . . . The crusts of snow . . . The walls that were beginning to rise up across the way, the girders in which wire stems were set before the concrete was poured.

It was five in the afternoon, and he had done everything that he had to do, his marketing, his cooking, his dishes. He had dozed in the armchair in the living room until semidarkness had set in, and he had seen Marguerite sitting in her place.

She was as motionless as the parrot. . . . She did not look at him. . . . They had stopped looking at each other long ago. . . .

He walked. . . . He felt the need for fresh air. . . .

He had had a drink in a café. . . . He was never drunk, but he drank, he drank a lot. . . . He had better control himself.

"The bitches."

He was not thinking of anyone. It was mechanical. . . . The words recurred to him from time to time, like an incantation. . . .

When they still spoke to each other, in a distant past, Marguerite would murmur when he least expected it:

"Jesus, Mary, Joseph . . ."

And as he expressed surprise, she explained to him that she thereby acquired three hundred days of indulgence, three hundred days, if he understood correctly, that she would not have to spend in Purgatory.

He could have gone to Nelly's. She would have looked at him with a compassionate smile, for he had aged even more. Would he still have had the desire, the strength, to go behind the kitchen door with her?

Two years? . . . Three years? . . .

The fact is, he no longer knew. People went God knows where. Their comings and goings had no meaning, nor did the lighted shopwindows, which were depressing, since nobody looked at them because of the wind. . . .

In the movies, people sat motionless, in rows, looking at photographs that moved. . . .

It was he who was tired. He had expected it. Women have more endurance. The statistics were right. . . .

When Angèle . . .

No, it was Nelly . . . But a Nelly who had Marguerite's smile. . . .

Actually, they all had the same smile, a smile that meant that they would end by winning out. . . .

. . . with her big hat and princess dress, a parasol in her hand, on the riverbank. . . .

It was she who had told him that the dress was called a princess dress. He had seen them in the street, a long long time ago. . . .

Cochin Hospital . . . Farther off, to the right, the prison . . . Between the two, the alley, which now had only one row of houses and where one was surprised to see from a distance windows that were lighted. . . .

There were no lights in his house, that is, in Marguerite's house. He took the key from his pocket. He nervously opened the door in the darkness and silence.

He switched on the light and entered the living room. Nobody. The knitting on the floor. Nobody in the dining room, or the kitchen either. He went up as fast as he could. She had probably gone out on purpose, to give him a fright.

"Mar . . ."

He was about to call her by name, forgetting that they did not speak to each other.

He opened the door. . . . He put on the light. And there she was, on the rug, as he expected to find her. . . .

The sight did not surprise him. What was curious was that she had undone her bed and taken off her dress. Death had struck her in her slip. . . .

Had she called out? Had she uttered his name in the emptiness of the house without an answering voice?

He was seized with panic, went down the stairs, left the

house without thinking of closing the door, and walked quickly to the corner of Boulevard Arago where Dr. Burnier lived. Bouin had never seen him. The doctor did not come to the house, but one day when Emile was following Marguerite, he had seen her enter the building and he had read his name on the plaque.

He rang and rang. . . .

"What is it? The doctor isn't . . ."

A dark-skinned servant with a heavy foreign accent. A discreetly lighted marble entrance hall.

"My wife . . ."

"I told you that the doctor . . ."

"But . . . It's my wife. . . ."

She tried to close the door, but, as she looked at him, she suddenly changed her mind.

"What's the matter with you?"

"Nothing. . . . It's my . . ."

He staggered forward. At the left was a Louis XVI bench covered with faded pink velvet, like one of the dresses . . .

The fog enveloping him also was pink.

When he opened his eyes, he saw at first only whiteness. It seemed to him that there was sunlight. Turning his head slightly, he distinguished beds, faces.

"Don't move."

He tried to look the other way and succeeded. A gray-haired nurse was holding his wrist in one hand and a watch in the other.

"Sh . . ."

She was counting, moving her lips, silently, the way Marguerite counted her stitches.

"Ma . . ."

"Sh . . ."

"Where . . ."

"Lie still. Don't be afraid. You're at the hospital, and we're taking care of you. . . . The professor will be here shortly."

The word "professor" made him wonder where he was—at school? He didn't have all his wits about him. His body was so numb that the nurse laid his hand on the bed without his feeling it.

"My wife . . ."

"I know. . . . It's been attended to. . . ."

The professor . . . Attended to . . . Attended to what? . . .

He found the strength to say: "But she's dead."

He thought he was screaming, and his voice could hardly be heard.

"Be quiet. . . . Here he comes."

She stood up in relief and spoke in a low voice to a middle-aged man in a white smock. They both were looking at him.

"Do you feel like vomiting?"

He did not know. He felt nothing. It was somewhat as if his body no longer belonged to him.

No nausea or sharp pains . . .

His left hand felt his chest, and he was surprised to find a rigid bandage under his fingers.

"You underwent an emergency operation last night. . . . Above all, you mustn't move."

"My wife . . ."

"It's being attended to. . . ."

"She's . . ."

"Yes. . . ."

"What about me?"

The doctor could not refrain from smiling.

"You'll live, but I won't hide from you the fact that you'll be here a long time. . . . You'll have to be patient. . . ."

He promised. He had always been patient. He would be patient as long as they liked, as long as they allowed him to be.

He was . . . It was hard to think. The doctor's smile . . . There was . . . He tried to find the word. . . . He did not find it. . . . There was no longer anything . . .

Epalinges, October 5, 1966